Serapion by Francis Stevens

A pseudonym of Gertrude Barrows Bennett

Gertrude Barrows Bennett was born in Minneapolis on 18th September 1884.

She completed school up to the eighth grade, then switched to night school to study illustration, unfortunately she was never able to achieve a career in this. As a fall-back she began working as a stenographer, a career which she would keep to for the rest of her life.

But Gertrude had talent, writer's talent. Her first short story was written when she was 17. Not you would think the usual subjects of curious teenage girls with headstrong ambitions but a science fiction story entitled 'The Curious Experience of Thomas Dunbar'. She mailed the finished story to Argosy, one of the most well known of the pulp magazines. The story was published in the March 1904 issue.

Whilst her career was to be short and not at all prolific she is best remembered for her excellent ideas, many of which were way ahead of their time. By the time of her death in 1948 her pseudonym of 'Francis Stevens' could lay claim to being a respected and much admired author of science fiction and dark fantasy short stories and novels.

Index of Contents

CHAPTER I

It began because, meeting Nils Berquist in town one August morning, he dragged me off for luncheon at a little restaurant on a side street where he swore I would meet some of the rising geniuses of the century.

What we did meet was the commencement for me of such an extraordinary experience as befalls few men. At the time, however, the whole affair seemed incidental, with a spice of grotesque but harmless absurdity. Jimmy Moore and his Alicia! How could anyone, meeting them as I did, have believed a grimness behind their amusing eccentricity?

I was just turned twenty-four that August day. A boy's guileless enthusiasm for the untried was still strong in me, coupled with a tendency to make friends in all quarters, desirable or otherwise. Almost anyone who liked me, I liked. My college years, very recently ended, had seen me sworn comrade to a reckless and on-his-way-to-be-notorious son of plutocracy, while I was also well received in the room which Nils Berquist sharing with two other embryo socialists of fanatic dye. A certain ingenuous likableness must have been mine even then, I think, to have gained me not only toleration, but real friendship in both camps.

Berquist was older than I by several years. He had earned his college days before enjoying them and, college ended, he dropped back into the struggle for existence and out of my sight—till I ran across him in town that August day.

To play host even at a very moderate luncheon must have been an extravagance for Nils, though I didn't think of that. He was a man with whom one somehow never associated the idea of need. Tall, lean, with a dark, long face, high cheekbones and deep eyes set well apart, he dressed badly and walked the world in a careless air of ownership that mere clothes could not in the least affect.

His intimates knew him capable of vast, sudden enthusiasms, and equally vast depressions of the spirit. But up or down, he was Nils Berquist, sufficient unto himself, asking no favors, and always with an indefinable air of being well able to grant them.

I admired and liked him, was very glad to see him again, and cheerfully let him steer me around two corners and in the door of his bragged-of trysting place.

On first entering, my friend cast an eye about the aggregation of more or less shabby individuals present and muttered: "Not a soul here!" in a disappointed tone. Then, glimpsing a couple seated at a corner table laid for four, he brightened a trifle and led me over to them.

Nil's idea of formal presentation was always more brief than elaborate. After addressing the fair-haired, light-eyelashed, Palm-Beach-suited person on one side of the table as "Jimmy" and his vis-a-vis, a darkly mysterious lady in a purple veil, as "Alicia," he referred to me casually as "Clay," and considered the introduction complete.

I do not mean that the lady's costume was limited to the veil. Only that this article was of such peculiar, brilliantly, fascinatingly ugly hue that the rest of her might have been clothed in anything from a mermaid's scales to a speckled calico wrapper; I can image nothing except a gown of the same color which would have distracted one's attention from that veil.

The thing was draped over a small hat and hung all about her head and face in a sort of circular curtain. Behind it I became aware of two dark bright eyes watching me, like the eyes of some sea creature, laired behind a highly futurist wave. Having met peculiar folk before in Berquist's company, I took a seat opposite the veil without embarrassment.

"Charming little place, this," I lied, glancing about the low-ceilinged semi ventilated, architectural container for chairs, tables and genius which formed a background to the veil. "Sorry I didn't discover it earlier."

The dark eyes gleamed immovably from their lair. I essayed a direct question. "You lunch here frequently, I presume?"

No answer. The veil didn't so much as quiver. Even my genial amity began to suffer a chill.

Suddenly "Jimmy" of the Palm Beach suit transferred his attention from Berquist to me. "Please don't try to talk with Alicia," he said. "She is in the silence today. If you draw her out it will disturb the vibrations for a week and make the deuce of a hole in my work. Do you mind?"

With a slight gasp I adjusted myself to the unusual. I said I didn't mind anything.

"You're the right sort, then. Might have known it, or you wouldn't be traveling with old man Nils, eh? What you going to have? Nothing worth eating except the broiled bluefish, and that's scorched. Always is. What you eating, Nils?"

"Rice," said Berquist briefly.

"On the one-dish-at-a-time diet, eh? Great stuff, if you can stick it out. Make an athlete out of a centenarian—if you can stick it out. Bluefish for one or two?" he added, addressing the waiter and myself in the same sentence.

"Two," I smiled. Palm Beach Jimmy seemed to have usurped my friend's role of host with calm casualism. The man's blond hair and faintly yellow lashes and eyebrows robbed his face of emphasis, so that the remarkably square and sloping forehead did not impress one at first. His way of assuming direction of even the slightest affairs about him struck me as easy-going and careless, rather than domineering.

He gave the rest of the order, with an occasional kindly reference to my desires. "And boiled rice for one," he finished.

The waiter cast a curious glance at the purple veil. "Nothing for the lady?" he queried.

"Seaweed, of course," retorted Jimmy. "You're new at this table, aren't you?"

"Just started working here. Seaweed, sir?"

"Certainly. There it is, staring you in the face under 'Salads.' Study your menu, man. That," explained Jimmy, after the waiter's somewhat dazed departure, "is the only reason we come here. One place I know of that serves rhodymenia serrata. Great stuff. Rich in mineral salts and vitamins."

"You didn't order any for yourself," I ventured.

"No. Great stuff, but has a horrid taste. Simply horrid! Alicia eats it as a martyr to the cause. We have to be careful of her diet. Very careful; Nils, old man, what's the new wrong to the human race you're being so silent over?"

"Can't say without becoming personal," retorted Berquist calmly.

"What? Oh, I forgot you don't approve. Still clinging to the sacred barriers, eh?"

"The barriers exist, and they are sacred." Nils' long, dark face was solemn, but as he was capable of cracking the wildest jokes with just that solemn expression, I wasn't sure if the conversation were light or serious. I only knew that as yet I had failed to get a grip on the situation. The man talked about his seaweed-fed Alicia as if the lady were not present.

What curiosity in human shape did that veil hide? One thing I was uneasily aware of. Not once, since the moment of our arrival had those laired bright eyes strayed from my face.

"The barriers exist," Berquist repeated. "I do not believe that you or others like you can tear them down. If I did, I should be justified in taking your life, as though you were any other dangerous criminal. When those barriers go down, chaos will swallow the world, and the race of men be superseded by the race of madmen!"

Jimmy laughed, unstartled by my friend's reference to cold-blooded assassination. "In the world of science," he retorted, "what one can do, one may do. If every investigator of novel fields had stopped his work for fear of scorched fingers—"

"In the material, physical world," interrupted Berquist, speaking in the same solemn, dogmatic tone, "what one can do, one may do. There, the worst punishment of a step too far can be only the loss of life or limb. It isn't man's rightful workshop. Let him learn its tools at the cost of a cut or so. But the field that you would invade is forbidden."

"By whom? By what?"

"By its nature! A man who risks his life may be a hero, but what is the name for a man who risks his soul?"

"Oh, Nils—Nils! You anachronism! You—you inquisitor! Here! You say the physical world is open ground—don't you?"

"Yes."

"And what is commonly referred to as the 'supernatural' is forbidden?"

"In the sense we speak of—yes."

"Very well. Now, where do you draw the fine dividing line? How do you know that your soul, as you call it, isn't just another finer form of matter? A good medium Alicia here can do it—stretches out a tenuous arm, a misty, wraithy, seimiformless limb, and lifts a ten-pound weight off the table while the 'physical' hands and feet are bound so they can't stir an inch. Telekinesis, that is called, or levitation, and you talk about it as if it were done by some sort of supernatural will power.

"Will power, yes; but will actuating matter to move matter. That fluidic arm is just as 'material.' though not so substantial, as your own husky biceps. It's thinner—different. But material—of course it's material! Why, you yourself are a walking case of miraculous levitation. Will moving matter. Will, a super physical force generated on the physical plane. Where's your fine dividing line? You talk about the material plane—"

"I won't any more," broke in Berquist hastily. "But you know that there are entities and forces dangerous to the human race outside of what we call the natural world, and that your investigations are no better than a sawing at the bars of a cage full of tigers. If I thought you could loose them, I have already told what I would do!"

There was a dark gleam in Berquist's deep-set eyes that suddenly warned me he meant exactly what he said—though the meaning of the whole argument was as hazy to me as the face behind that astounding veil.

Jimmy himself looked sober. "Here comes your rice," he said shortly. "Eat it, you old vegetarian, and get off the murder subject. I'll expect you to be coming around some night with a carving knife, if you say much more."

"There are police to guard you from the carving knife. The wild marches between this world and the invisible are patrolled by no police. Yet you fear the knife; which can harm only your body, and fearlessly expose your naked soul!"

"Thanks, old man, but my soul is well able to take care of itself. Eat your rice. There! Didn't I say the bluefish would be scorched? And it is. Behold, a prophet among you!"

The bluefish wasn't worrying me. What I was awaiting was the moment when that miraculously colored veil should be uplifted. Surely, her purple screen removed, the lady would cease to stare me out of countenance.

Before the veil a large platter of straggling, saw-edged, brownish-red leaves had been set down. The dish looked as horrid as Jimmy said it tasted. In a quiver of impatience I waited. At last I should see—a hand, white and well shaped, but slender to emaciation, was raised to the veil's lower edge. The edge was lifted. Another hand conveyed a modest forkful of the uncanny edible upward. It passed behind the veil. The fork came away empty.

With a gasping sigh I relinquished hope, and turned my attention to scorched bluefish.

Jimmy may have noted my emotion. "When Alicia is in the silence," he offered, "she has to be guarded. The vibratory rhythm of the violet light waves is less harmful than the rest of the spectrum. Hence, the veil. Invention of my own. You agree with our wild anarchist here, Mr.—er—Clay? Sacred barrierist and all that?"

"My name's Barbour," I said. "Clayton S. Barbour. As for the barriers, I must admit you've been talking over my head."

"So? Don't believe it. Pardon me, but your head doesn't look that sort. Hasn't Nils told you what I'm doing?"

"Nils," said Berquist, with what would have been cold insolence from anyone else, "has something better to do than walk about the world exploiting you to his acquaintances.

"I'm smashed—crushed flat," laughed Jimmy. He seemed one of the most good-humored individuals I had ever met. "Never mind, anarchist. I'll tend to it myself." He turned again to me. "Come to think of it, one of Nils' introductions is an efficient disguise. I'm James Barton Moore."

I murmured polite gratification. For the life of me I couldn't recall hearing the name before. His perception was as quick as his good humor. That ready laugh broke out again.

"Never heard of me, eh? That's a fault of mine—expect the whole world to be thrillingly expectant of results from my work. Ever hear of the Psychic Research Association?"

"Certainly." I looked as intelligent as possible. "Investigate ghosts and haunted houses and all that, don't they?"

"You're right, son. Ghosts and haunted houses about cover the Association's metier. Bah! Do you know who I am?"

"A member?" I hazarded.

"Not exactly. I'm the man the Association forced off its directing board. And I'm also the man who is going to make the Association look like; a crowd of children hunting spooks in the nursery. Come around to my place tonight and I'll show you something!"

The invitation was so explosively abrupt that I started in my chair.

"Why—er—" I began.

Nils broke in again. "Don't go," he said, coolly.

"Let him alone!" enjoined Moore, but with no sign of irritation. "You drop in around seven—here," he scribbled an address on the back of a card and tossed it across the table, "and I'll promise you an interesting evening."

"You are very good," I said, not knowing quite what to do. I already had an engagement for that evening; on the other hand, my ever-ready curiosity had been aroused.

"Don't go," repeated Berquist tonelessly.

"Thanks, but I believe I will."

"Good! You're the right sort. Knew it the minute I set eyes on you. Don't extend these invitations to everyone. Not by any means."

Berquist pushed back his chair.

"Are you going on with me, Clay?" he inquired.

I thought he was carrying his peculiar style of rudeness rather beyond the boundaries; but he was really my host, so I acquiesced. I took pains, however, to bid a particularly courteous farewell to the eccentric pair with whom we had lunched. I might or might not keep my appointment with Moore, but if I did I wished to be sure of a welcome.

With me the influence of a personality, however strong, ended where its line of direction crossed the course of my own wishes. Nils' opposition to my further acquaintance with the Moores had struck me as decidedly officious.

Once outside the restaurant, he turned on me almost savagely.

"Clay," he said, "you are not going up there tonight!"

"No?" I asked coldly. "And why not?"

"You don't know what you might be let in for. That is why not."

"You have an odd way of talking about your friends."

"Oh, Moore knows what I think."

"All right," I grinned, not really wishing a quarrel if one could be avoided. "But your friends are good enough for me, too, Nils. Who was the lady in the veil?"

"His wife. A physical medium. Heaven help her!"

"Spirit rapping, clairvoyant and all that, eh? I supposed it was something of the sort. Well, if I wish to go out to their place and spend a dollar or so to watch some conjuring tricks, why do you object so strenuously? That's one thing I've never done—"

"Spend a dollar or so!" snapped Berquist. "Those people are not professionals, Clay. Mrs. Moore is one of the few genuine mediums in this country."

"Oh, come! Surely you're not a believer in table-tipping and messages from Marcus Aurelius and Shakespeare?"

Berquist squinted at me disgustedly.

"Heaven help me save this infant!" he muttered, taking no pains, however, that I shouldn't hear him. "Clay, you go home and stay among your own people. Jimmy Moore is a moderately good fellow, but in one certain line he's as voracious as a wolf and unscrupulous as a Corsican bandit. He told you that he didn't extend these invitations to everyone. That is strictly true. The fact that he extended one to you is proof sufficient that you should not accept. He saw in you something he's continually on the watch for. He would use you and wreck you without a scruple."

"How? What do you mean?"

"If I should tell you in what way, you would laugh and call it impossible. But, let me say something you can understand. Except casually, Moore is not a pleasant man to know. He would like people to believe that he was dropped from the administrative board of the Association because his investigations and inferences were too daring for even the extraordinary open types of mind which compose it. The, real reason was that he proved so violently, overbearingly quarrelsome that even they couldn't tolerate him."

Recalling Moore's impregnable good humor under Nils' own attacks, I began to wonder exactly what was the latter's object.

"I'm not going there to quarrel with him," I said.

"No; you're going to be used by him. Look at that unfortunate little wife of his, if you want a horrible example."

"You mean he'd obscure my classic features with a purple veil? There'll be a fight to the finish first, believe me!"

"Oh, that veil-vibration-seaweed business—that's all rot. Just freak results of freak theorizing. Froth and bubbles. It's the dark brew underneath that's dangerous."

"Witch's scene in Macbeth," I chuckled. "Fire burn and caldron bubble! We now see Mr. Jimmy Moore in his famous personation of Beelzebub—costume, one Palm Beach suit and a cheerful grin. Don't worry, Nils! I'll bolt through the window at the first whiff of brimstone."

"My child," said Berquist, very gently and slowly, "you have the joyous courage of ignorance. Alicia Moore is that rare freak, a real materializing medium—a producer of supernormal physical phenomena, as they are called. In other words, she is an open channel for forces which are neither understood nor recognized by the average civilized man. And Timmy Moore is that much more common freak, a fool who doesn't care whose fingers get burnt. The responsibility for having introduced you to those people is mine. As a personal favor, I now ask you to have nothing more to do with either of them."

"Nils, you're back in the dark ages, as Moore claimed. I never thought you'd fall for this spiritualistic bunk."

"Leave that. You are determined to keep the appointment?"

"Come with me, if you think I need a chaperon."

"No," he said soberly.

"Why not?"

"He wouldn't have me. Not when a seance is planned, and that is what he meant by an 'interesting evening.' I'm persona non-grata on such an occasion, because Alicia says her spirit guides don't like me—save the mark! If I tried to wedge in tonight there would be another row, and Heaven alone knows where the thing would end. I wish you'd stay away from there!"

"Do you mean," I asked slowly, and beginning to see new light on Nils' attitude, "that you have quarreled with Moore in the past?"

"My dear fellow, get this through your head if you can. It is impossible to know Moore very long and not quarrel with him—or be subjugated. You keep away."

I was growing a little sick of Nils' persistence.

"Softy. Fear I haven't your faith in the bodiless powers of evil, and I can't say Moore seemed such an appalling person. I'm going!"

Abruptly, without a word of answer or farewell, Berquist turned his back on me and swung off down street. Several times I had seen him end a conversation in that manner, and I knew why. By rights, he should have been the last man to criticize another man's temper.

But I knew, too, that Nils' wrath was likely as evanescent as sudden. He would be as friendly as ever next time we met, and even if he were not, I couldn't see why his anger or disapproval should afflict me greatly. Friends were too easily acquired for me to miss one.

I forgot him promptly and began wondering how my dissertation for the evening would be accepted by Roberta Whitingfield.

CHAPTER II

That afternoon I reached home to find Roberta herself on the veranda with my sister Catherine. Rather to my consternation, on hearing of the restaurant encounter, Bert promptly dubbed it, "The Adventure of the Awful Veiled One," and announced her intent to solve the mystery in my company. Catherine seconded the motion, calmly including herself in the party, but there I rebelled.

Roberta and I were to be married one of these days. She was mine to command me.

I had a vague idea of what Moore's invitation portended, and I knew what would happen if I took both those girls and anything unusual occurred. They would giggle.

We kept Roberta with us for dinner, and when she had gone home to dress, Cathy and I had our argument in earnest. My mother was confined to her room with one of her frequent headaches, and for a while dad hid himself in his paper. Then a grizzled head appeared over the top of it.

"Cathy," he drawled, "I haven't a notion what this is all about, but wherever Clay is off to, I'm sure he doesn't want two girls. Clay, I don't wish to be rude, but if you are going, won't you please depart at once? Run upstairs, Catherine, and see if all this loud talking has disturbed your mother."

Cathy went. She knew better than to oppose dad when he used that tone.

That evening I called for Roberta in my car, and after nine o'clock we arrived at the address written across Moore's card. It turned out to be half of a detached double dwelling, standing on a corner beyond a block of quiet, respectable red-stone fronts, with a deep lawn between it and the street.

"Ridiculous house," Bert named it on first sight, and ridiculous house it was in a certain sense. It reminded one of that king in the old fairy tale who "laughed with one side of his face and smiled with the other."

The half that bore Moore's number was neat, shining and of unimpeachable exterior. Its yellow brick front was clean, with freshly painted white woodwork; it's half of the lawn, close-clipped and green, was set with little thriving round flower beds.

The other half had the look of a regular old beggar among houses. The paint, weather-beaten, blistered and brown, was no dingier than the dirt-freckled bricks. Two or three windows were boarded up. Not one of the rest but mourned a broken pane or so. From the dilapidated porch wooden steps all askew led to a weed-grown walk. On that side the lawn was a straggling waste of weeds.

Roberta had hopped out of the car without waiting for assistance. I joined her and we stood staring at the queer-looking combination.

"Roberta," I said solemnly after a moment, "there is a grim, grisly secret which I hadn't meant to alarm you with, but perhaps it is better you should be warned now."

"Clay! What do you mean?"

"That house!" My voice was a sinister whisper. "Don't you see? 'Life and death,' or 'Chained to the corpse of his victim!' Moore murdered one of the twin houses, and now he must live in the other house as a penance."

To my surprise, instead of laughing at my nonsense, she took my arm with a shiver. "Don't!" she protested. "When you speak so the house isn't funny any more. It's horrid. A-a dead-alive house! Let's not go in, Clay."

I felt annoyed, for this last-moment retreat was not like her. I said, "Come along, Berty, and don't be silly. I suppose one half belongs to Moore and the other to somebody else, and he can't make the other owner keep his half in repair."

After some further discussion, we entered the gate at last. I remembered that as we went up Moore's walk, I threw back my head and glanced upward. The moonlight was so white on the slanting house roofs that for just a moment I had an illusion of their being thick with snow.

With snow. Yes, I remembered that illusion afterward.

Moore had expected me alone, of course, but he needn't have made that fact quite so obvious. He met us in his library on the second floor, whither a neat, commonplace maid had ushered us after a glance at my card.

It was a long, rather heavily furnished room, lined with books to the ceiling. Our first view of it noted nothing bizarre or out of the ordinary. Moore was seated reading, but as we were announced he rose quickly. It was when he perceived Roberta and realized that I had brought a companion that I had my first real doubt that Nils had not exaggerated about the man's temper.

His good-humored, full-lipped mouth seemed to draw inward and straighten to a disagreeably gash-like-effect. The skin over his cheekbones tightened. A pronounced narrowness between the eyes forced itself suddenly upon the attention. For one instant we faced a man disagreeably different from the one who had parried all Berquist's thrusts with unshakable good nature.

As he rose and came toward us, however, the ominous look melted again to geniality. "Began to think old Nils had seared you off in earnest, Barbour," he greeted. "Witch burnings; would still be in order if our wild anarchist had his way, eh?"

Rather reluctantly I performed the necessary introductions.

"I had no right to come with Clayton," Roberta apologized. "But when he told me of your invitation, I—we thought—"

"That you might find some amusement here?" Moore finished for her. "That's all right, Miss Whitingfield, though the work I am engaged in is a bit serious to be amusing, I fear. Hope you're not the nervous, screaming sort?" he added, with blunt anxiety.

She flushed a trifle, then laughed. "I'm not—really!" she protested. "But I'll go away if you wish."

That was too much for me. "We'll both leave," I said very haughtily. "Sorry to have put you out, Mr. Moore."

To my astonishment, for I was really angry, he burst out laughing. It was such a genial, inoffensive merriment as caught me unawares. I found myself laughing with him, though at what I hadn't the faintest notion.

"Why, Barbour," he chuckled, "you mustn't take offense at a lack of conventional mannerisms on my part. I'm a worker first, last and all the time. Miss Whitingfield, you're welcome as the flowers in May, but I can no more forget my work nor what is likely to affect it than I can forget my own name. You—aren't angry with me, are you?"

"N-no—" she began rather hesitatingly, but just then the door opened behind us and we heard someone enter.

"I am here!"

The words were uttered in a dry, toneless voice. We both turned, and I realized that the "Mystery of the Awful Veiled One" was a mystery no more, or at least had been shorn of its purple drapery.

Of course, I had expected to meet Alicia here, but I think I should have recognized those eyes in any surroundings. They were fully as bright, dark, and almost incredibly large and attentive as they had seemed behind the veil. For the rest, Mrs. Moore's slender figure was draped in filmy black, between which and a mass of black hair her face gleamed, a peaked white patch—and with those eyes in it.

"Medium" or not, Mrs. Moore herself was more like the creature of another world than any human being I had ever seen.

"Be seated, Alicia."

Without troubling to present Roberta, Moore gestured toward a peculiar-looking chair at one side of the room. The slender creature in black swept toward it obediently.

Having reached the chair, she turned, faced us for a moment, still expressionless save for those terribly attentive eyes, then sank into the chair's depths.

Roberta was frankly staring, and so was I, but my stare had a newly startled quality. Alicia had passed me very closely indeed. My hand still tingled where another hand—a bony, fierce little hand—had closed on it in a swift, pinching clasp. And though I was sure that her colorless lips had not moved, four low words had reached my ears distinctly.

"Go away—you! Go."

I glanced at Berty, but decided that she had missed the rude little message. Moore certainly hadn't heard, for he had gone over to the chair, and was standing behind it when Alicia reached there.

With a slight shrug I determined that where so much oddity prevailed, this additional eccentricity of Mrs. Moore had better be ignored. To think of her as a real person—my hostess—was made difficult by the atmosphere of utter strangeness which her appearance and Moore's treatment of her had already created.

"You and Miss Whitingfield sit over there," commanded Moore briskly.

"I'll explain what we're about in a minute. You'll be interested. Can't avoid it. A little farther off, Miss Whitingfield—do you mind? Alicia is more easily affected than other sensitives. More easily affected. Right! Now just a moment and I can talk to you."

We had seated ourselves as he directed, I some half dozen feet from the enthroned Alicia, Roberta much farther away, well over by the heavily curtained windows.

To the savage and to the young "strange" is generally synonymous with "funny." We exchanged one quick look, then kept our eyes resolutely apart. A wave of incipient mirth had fairly leaped between us. It was well, I thought, that Cathy had been suppressed.

Then we saw what Moore was doing at the chair, and forgot laughter in amazement. It must be remembered that Roberta and I were innocent of the least previous experience in this line. Save for some hazy knowledge of "spiritualistic fakes" and "mind-reading" of the vaudeville type, we were blankly ignorant, and by consequence as unconsciously receptive as a couple of innocent young sponges. But at first we were merely shocked by the brutal fact of Moore's preparations.

I have said that the chair taken by Alicia was a peculiar one. It stood before a pair of black curtains, which concealed what in spiritualistic circles is called a cabinet. The chair itself was large, heavy, with a high back and uncommonly broad armrests. More, it had about it that look of apparatus which one associates with dentists' and surgeons' fixtures. Alicia leaned back in it, her hands resting limp on the armrests.

Then up over each fragile wrist Moore clamped a kind of steel handcuff, attached to the chair arm. Another pair of similar fetters, extended on short rods from the back, were clasped round her upper arms. And, as if this were not enough—he locked together the two halves of a wide steel band about her waist.

And his wife sat there, inert as a porcelain doll, her enormous eyes wide open and fixed on me in perfectly unswerving contemplation.

"All really great mediums will trick you if they can," said Moore coolly. "Don't need any object for fraud. Unless you should call the trickery itself an object. Alicia is a great medium. Very—great!"

Suddenly every decent impulse I had rose to revolt. That was a woman in the chair—Moore's wife—and he treated her, talked about her, as though she were some peculiarly trained and subject animal.

I rose sharply. "Mrs. Moore, is this affair proceeding with your consent?"

"Don't address the psychic!" snapped her husband over one shoulder.

But I wasn't afraid of him. At that moment I could have thrashed the man cheerfully—and with ease, for I carried no superfluous flesh in those days, and had inches the better of him in height and reach. Roberta was suddenly at my side, and I knew—by the excited shine of her eyes—that she sensed my emotion and approved it.

"Mrs. Moore," I repeated "are you enduring this of your own free will? Moore, attempt to intimidate her, and you'll be sorry!"

He straightened, and turned on me in earnest, but Alicia herself broke the strain.

"Sit down, boy," she said in her dry, toneless voice. "What James says of fraud is true. But he does not mean what you think. I am not conscious of what I do in trance, and the self then in control has no moral standards. Were my earthly limbs not bound, no phenomena could be credited, and my own guides have advised the construction of the chair. The steel bands are padded with felt, and do not hurt me. I did not speak to you when I entered, because at some times the guides like me to be silent. This is tiring me. You must not quarrel with James. Violent emotion tires me. A great evil will come to you through me, but now you must sit down and be very quiet. I am tired."

For the first time, white lids drooped over those unnatural eyes. The closing of them seemed to rob her face of the last trace of fellow-humanity. Moore was grinning again, though rather tensely.

"Please sit down, Barbour," he pleaded in a very low voice. "I should have explained a few things to you in advance. Alicia will be asleep directly, and then we can talk."

I did sit down, and Roberta retired to her window. That toneless, indifferent voice of Alicia's, that cool exactitude of statement, had not seemed the expression of a meek and terrorized soul. But if she were not afraid of Moore, why had she been so surreptitious in asking—in ordering me to leave? "I did not speak to you when I entered—" But she had spoken to me. "A great evil will come to you through me—" And she said it like a remark on the weather!

I gave up suddenly. All my curiosity was submerged in a wave of healthy revolt against the obviously abnormal. A vague unhappiness came with it, and the desire above everything to take Roberta and get out.

Alicia was breathing regularly now, in long, deep breaths, soft but audible. Leaving her, Moore drew up a chair between Roberta and me, seated himself, crossed one leg over his knee, and beamed amiably.

"Mr. Moore," I began, but he checked me, finger in air.

"Sh! Trifle lower, please. I know what you're thinking, Barbour, and I don't blame you. Not in-the-least! My fault entirely. Now let's drop all that and forget it. You are two very intelligent people, but I can never remember that the average man or woman knows as much about sensitives as a baby knows of trigonometry. Now, why did I invite you here, Barbour?"

"For an interesting evening, you said."

"Exactly! And you'll have it. First of many, I hope. But don't expect any messages from your deceased grandfathers tonight, for you won't get 'em."

"Very well," I assented. "Bert, do you hear that? Our revered ancestors won't speak to us!"

"And don't imagine this is a matter for joking, either," reproved Moore, but still amiably. "I did not say that purely spiritual forces would not be involved. But a psychic—a medium—has all the complexity of the highest type of nervous human—plus. And it's the plus sign that complicates matters. You might get messages through from almost anyone—eventually. You'll seem to get them tonight. But they won't be real. Alicia has more different selves than the proverbial cat has lives. And all wanting a chance to talk, and parade around, and pass themselves off as anybody you'd care to name, from Julius Caesar to your mother's deceased aunt's nephew. Very remarkable!"

"I should say so!"

We glanced rather anxiously at Alicia's quiescent figure. But no sudden procession of selves had yet appeared.

"That, however, is beside the mark," announced Moore briskly. "In such commonplace manifestations, Alicia dematerializes a percentage of her own fleshly bulk, externalizes and projects it from her subliminal consciousness. Aside from proving the accepted laws of matter to be false, the phenomena are of small importance."

He paused again.

"I should think," ventured Roberta, carefully avoiding my eyes, "that disproving the laws of matter would be—might be almost enough for one evening."

"The accepted laws," he corrected rather sharply. "Crooks-Oschorowicz-Lombroso-Bottazzi-Lodge—I could name you over a dozen great scientists who have already disproved them in that way. But they had only Tusapia Paladino and lesser psychics to work with. We have—Alicia!"

A vague memory stirred in me. "Paladino?" I said. "You mean that famous Italian medium? I thought she was exposed as a fraud."

He frowned. This was a sore subject with him, though I did not know why till much later.

"I tell you," he scowled, "they are all frauds—when they have the chance. The first impulse of hysteria is toward deception. Genuine mediumship and hysteria are practically inseparable. What can you expect? Paladino was as genuine as Alicia, and Alicia will fool you outrageously, given the least opportunity. Quite—scandalously—unscrupulous!"

"You're very frank about it," I couldn't help saying.

"Why not? You heard Alicia's own statement in that regard. She works with me to overcome the disadvantage. Mabel and Maudie are manageable enough, but Horace is a born joker. For a long time Horace fought bitterly against the idea of that chair, and only yielded when I threatened to give up the sittings."

"These people are friends who attend the seances?" I inquired, thinking that Moore had Nils' habit of referring to all his acquaintances by their Christian names.

Moore appeared mildly surprised.

"Don't you really know anything at all of spiritualistic investigation?"

"Sorry. I'm afraid I've never had enough faith in spooks to be interested."

"Never mind. We'll correct that!" assured Moore calmly. "Mabel and Maudie and Horace are three of Alicia's spirit guides. She believes them to be real entities of the spirit world—people who have passed beyond, you understand—but I doubt it. Doubt it—very seriously! In fact, I have reason to be positive that those three, along with several subsidiary 'spirits,' are just so many phases of Alicia's subconscious. On the other band, Jason Gibbs, her real 'control,' is a spirit to be reckoned with. You will find Jason an amazingly interesting man on acquaintance. And now that I have explained fully, suppose we take a look at the cabinet?"

Roberta and I rose and followed him, not sure whether to be amused or impressed. His statement that he had "explained fully" was a joke, so far as we were concerned. What nebulous ideas of a seance we had possessed were far removed from anything we had met tonight. To sit in a circle, holding hands in the dark; to hear mysterious raps and poundings; to glimpse, perhaps, the cheese-clothy forms of highly fictitious "ghosts"—that had been our previous conception of a "sitting" culled from general and half-forgotten reading.

Moore was so utterly matter-of-fact and unmystical of manner that he probably impressed us more deeply than if he had attempted to inspire awe.

And, I reflected, if he were a charlatan, where was his profit? Nils himself had assured me that Mrs. Moore was not a professional medium.

The fact was that I had emerged from college almost wholly ignorant of the modern debate between the physicist and the spiritist—ignorant that science itself had been driven to admission of supernormal powers in certain "victims of hysteria," but stood firm on the ground that these powers were of physical and terrestrial origin.

James Barton Moore, however, was a born materialist who had accepted the spiritistic theory from an intellectual viewpoint. The result showed in his matter-of-fact way of dealing with the occult. He had, moreover, one characteristic of a certain type of scientist in less weird fields. He would have put a stranger or his best friend on the vivisection table, could he by that means have hoped to acquire one small modicum of the knowledge he sought.

Figuratively, he already had me on the table that night.

CHAPTER III

On pushing aside the black curtains, the cabinet proved to be a place like a square closet, with a smooth, solid wooden back, built out from the wall. In it there stood a small, rather heavy table, made of polished oak, on which reposed several objects.

There was a thing like a small megaphone, to which Moore referred as the "cone." There was an ordinary glass tumbler, nearly filled with water; a lump of soft putty; a sheet of paper blackened by sooty smoke; a pad of ordinary white paper, and several pencils and pens, of different colors and sizes.

"Our preparations tonight," said Moore, "are of the simplest sort. I have passed the stage of registering Alicia's externalized motivity by means of instruments of precision. The exact force exerted to lift a weight yards beyond her bodily reach, the regulated rhythm of a metronome's pendulum, compression of a pneumatic ten feet from her hand—these have all been proved and left behind me. Others have done that with other mediums.

"But I go the step further that Bottazzi and many others dared not take. Having admitted the phenomena, I admit a cause for them outside the physical and beyond Alicia's individuality. I admit the disembodied spirit. My experiments are no longer based on doubt, but certainty. Their culmination will mean a revolution for the thinking world—a reversal of its whole stand toward matter and the forces that affect it."

Roberta and I were not particularly interested in revolutions of thought. Like younger children, we wished to know what he proposed doing with the things on the table, and after that we wished to see it done. So we stood silent, hoping that he would stop talking soon and let the exhibition of Alicia's mysterious powers begin.

Being off on his hobby, Moore probably mistook our silence for interest. At last, however, in the midst of a dissertation on "psychic force," "telekinesis" and "spiritual controls," he was interrupted by a long, deep sigh from the chair. The sigh was followed by a strangled gasping, very much as though Alicia were choking to death.

We both started toward the chair, but Moore barred the way.

"Let her alone!" he ordered imperatively. "She's all right. Come back to your seats." And when we had returned to our former positions, he added: "She is going into trance now. Later you may approach closer—hold her hands, if you like. But Alicia can't bear even myself to be very near her in the first stages. It hurts her, you understand. Gives her physical pain."

Judging from poor Alicia's appearance, she was in physical pain anyway. Her peaked white face writhed in the most unpleasant contortions. She choked, gasped, gurgled and showed every symptom of a woman in dying agonies. Then suddenly she quieted, her face resumed its lay-figure calmness, and the great eyes opened wide.

"Differs from most psychics. Opens her eyes in trance. Quite frequently." I heard Moore muttering; but Alicia herself began to speak now, and I forgot him.

The queerest, silliest little voice issued from her lips. It was like a child's voice, but an idiot child's.

"Pretty, pretty, pretty!" it gurgled. "Oh such a pretty lady! Did pretty lady come to see Maudie?" Followed a pause. When it spoke again the voice had a petulant note: "Did pretty lady come to see Maudie?"

Moore looked at Roberta. "Why don't you answer her, Miss Whitingfield?"

Before she could comply, however, another personality had apparently superseded the idiot child. A great laugh that I would have sworn was a man's echoed across the silent library. It seemed to come from Alicia's throat.

"Ha, ha, ha! Oh, ha, ha! You've got queer taste, Jimmy Moore! Why do you want to drag that pair of freaks in here? Tell 'em to go home! Go on home, young fellow, d'you hear? Go on, now—and take the skirt with you!"

"That is Horace," commented Moore imperturbably. "You haven't any manners, Horace, have you?"

"Not a manner!" retorted the voice. "Is that young sport going to leave, or do I have to heave a brick at him? Scat! Get out—you!"

This was certainly outside my idea of a seance. It occurred to me abruptly that the voice was not proceeding from Alicia. Some confederate was concealed nearby—had entered the cabinet, perhaps, by a concealed door. Or Moore himself was ventriloquizing.

Then I realized that Alicia's eyes were again fixed on my face, and their expression was not that of a woman entranced. They were keen, bright, intelligent. Her lips moved.

"Get! Get out!" adjured that brutally vulgar voice. Then it changed to a whining, female treble: "You are young, Clayton Barbour; young and soft to the soft, cruel hand that would mold you. You are easy to mold as clay-clay-Clayton-clay! Evil hangs over you—black evil! Flee from the damned Clayton Barbour. Go home—you!"

Moore was frowning uneasily.

"Subliminal," he said shortly. "Pay no attention to these voices. They emanate from the subconscious—Alicia's dream self. Similar to delirium, you know."

"Ah!" I murmured, and settled back in my chair. Not that I agreed with Moore, though I had dismissed thought of either a confederate or my host's ventriloquism. The ventriloquist was Alicia herself. I had no doubt that she could have caused the voices to sound from any quarter of the room as easily as from her own throat. As for trance, her eyes were entirely too wakeful and intelligent. Nearly everything said so far had been more repetition, in different phrases and voices, of that first brief, fierce little demand that I leave.

But by that time I was more than a trifle annoyed. It was hardly pleasant to sit in Roberta's presence and hear rude puns made on my name—to bear it implied that I was a mere nonentity with no character of my own. I rather plumed myself that Alicia would not find me so pliable. If she really wished me to depart, she had gone the wrong way about it.

"Ah," I said, settled back, and—the vulgarity of "Horace" may have been contagious—deliberately winked at Alicia. It was a crude enough act, but her methods struck me as crude, too.

A blaze of fury leaped into those too attentive eyes. Her features writhed in such an abominable convulsion as I had never believed possible to the human countenance. Purple, distorted, terrible—with a flashing of bone-white teeth—and out of it all a voice discordant, and different from any we had heard.

"Fool-fool-fool!" it grated. "Protect—try—can't protect fool! Slipping—it's got me—I'm slip-Oh-h-h! Oh-h-h-h!"

Even Moore seemed affected this time. We were all on our feet, and he was beside his wife in three long strides. As the last, long-drawn moan died away, however, the dreadful purple subsided from Alicia's countenance as quickly as it had risen. She was again the queer, white porcelain doll, leaning back with closed lids in her imprisoning chair.

Moore straightened, wiped his forehead, and laughed shakily.

"Do you know," he said, "with all the experience I've had, Alicia still gives me an occasional fright? But I never saw her pass into the second stage quite so violently."

"Don't these horrible convulsions hurt your wife, Mr. Moore?"

Roberta was deeply distressed, and no wonder! I felt as if I had brought her to watch the seizures of an epileptic.

"She says they don't," replied Moore. "But never mind that. Listen!"

Alicia's lips writhed whitely. "Light!" came her barely audible whisper.

Promptly Moore reached for a switch. Two of the three lights burning went out. The third was a shaded library lamp on a table not far off. I expected him to extinguish that also, for everything in the room was plainly visible, but he let it be.

"You may hold Alicia's hands, if you wish," he offered generously.

We shook our heads. Presently the hushed whisper was heard again.

"Many shadows are here tonight," it said. "Shadows living and dead. They crowd close. An old, old shadow comes. Blood runs from his lean, gnarled throat. He speaks!"

The whisper became a ghastly, bubbling attempt at articulation. There were no words. The result was just an abominable sound.

"Man with his throat cut might speak like that," observed Moore reflectively. "She must mean old Jenkins, who was murdered next door. That's the reason we have this house, you know. The other half's supposed to be haunted—and is."

Now I wanted to get out in earnest. Fraud or epileptic, Alicia was entirely too horrible, and Moore, with his calmness, almost worse. I tried to draw Roberta toward the door, but she held back.

"Not yet, Clay. I wish to see what will happen."

Now the horrid gurgle had merged into a man's voice. It was loud and distinct as "Horace's," but otherwise slightly different—as different, say, as tenor from high baritone.

"I am Jason Gibbs," it asserted. "Mr. Moore, will you kindly ask your friends to step back a little? We will do what we can for you, but my fellow spirits are a trifle shy of strangers."

Moore motioned us back. At the same time he shook his head smilingly.

"That's not Jason," he murmured. "A very good imitation, but an imitation, nonetheless. We shan't get much tonight."

"And in that," retorted the tenor, "you are exactly mistaken! You will get much. In fact you are likely to get more than one of you ever bargained for. You say I'm not Jason Gibbs? Seeing is believing, isn't it? Shall I show myself?"

Moore acquiesced smoothly. "Do so, by all means."

"I'll attend to that in a little while. I can read your mind all right, Jimmy Moore! You think I'm Horace talking high. Well, Horace is a very good fellow, and fond of his joke, but I'm Jason Gibbs tonight—and all the time, of course! Like to see something pretty?"

"Anything at all, Hor—pardon me Jason!"

"Then watch the cabinet."

We did. For a minute or two nothing happened.

Then Roberta cried out: "It's on fire!"

"No," said Moore. "Watch!"

A strange, tiny flame was running along the edge of the black curtains where they touched the floor.

When I say "running along," I do not mean that in the usual sense as applied to fire. It was a tiny, individual flame, violet in color, about an inch and a half high, and as it moved it twirled and spun on its own base in the oddest manner. Reaching the center, where the curtains joined, it floated slowly upward, still twirling, left the cabinet and presently disappeared, apparently through the ceiling. Another flame and another followed it.

I assured myself that we were watching a very clever and unusual exhibition of fireworks. But I didn't believe that. I didn't know exactly what I believed, but I did know that those twirling, violet flames were the first really strange thing I had ever seen in my life. When seven of them had appeared and vanished, Moore spoke.

"Isn't that enough—er Jason? Can't you do better than that for us?"

There was silence, while the eighth and last flame twirled upward and vanished. Then, that great, rough laugh burst startlingly from Alicia's lips.

"Ha. Ha, ha! Ha, ha! Oh, Jimmy Moore, I should say I can do better! I should say so!"

And with that the curtains parted suddenly and—it is hard to tell, but it was harder to stand the shock of it—a huge, misshapen, grayish-black hand darted out from between them.

Behind it I caught a glimpse of wrist—I couldn't see any arm. It just leaped out and into existence, as one might say, and to my unspeakable horror laid its gross, gnarled fingers fairly across Roberta Whitingfield's mouth and chin.

I believed it had seized her throat. Half-mad with shock, I sprang at the hand, gripping, holding it in both of mine. I felt a kind of roughness in my grasp—a rough solidity that melted to nothing even as I touched it. My hands were empty. I caught Roberta, as she swayed backward, whiter than Alicia herself.

And Moore was reproving—something, in the most everyday manner.

"Really, Horace, that wasn't a nice joke at all!" he criticized.

Easing Roberta into a chair, I sprang savagely at the curtains and swept them aside: behind there was only the table and what we had seen on it. I had a fleeting impression that the lump of putty was different—that, where it had been a formless lump, it appeared now as if it had been squeezed between giant fingers. Then Moore was pulling me back.

"Don't do that, Barbour. We shan't get anything more, if you interfere like that."

"Devil!" it was all I could think of to call him, and it seemed inadequate enough.

"You—devil! To play a trick like that on an unsuspecting girl! Bert, darling, come, I'll take you home; then I'll come back and settle with these people!"

"Barbour, I give you my word of honor that I had nothing to do with what just occurred. You brought Miss Whitingfield here of your own volition, and pardon me—against my wishes. But she assured me she was, not of the nervous type—"

"Nervous!" I repeated scornfully. "A really nervous woman would have died when that black paw flew out at her!"

"I'm not hurt, Clayton," intervened Roberta. "Don't quarrel with him—please!"

"You are sensible," approved Moore, "There is no danger from such manifestations as that hand. Why, I have taken a peek into the cabinet when the power was strong and seen half a dozen human limbs and parts of limbs lying about—fragmentary impulses, as one might say, of the mediumistic force—"

But here, with marked decision, Roberta rose.

"I think we will go home, Clay. I have just discovered that I am of the nervous, screaming sort! Mr. Moore, will you please say good night for us to Mrs. Moore when she—when she wakens?"

He sighed disappointedly.

"It's too bad, really! If Jason Gibbs had actually been in control tonight there would have been nothing to shock you. Horace is nothing. Just a secondary, practical-looking phase of Alicia's own personality."

"Come, Roberta." We started toward the door.

And then, without a warning flicker, the library lamp went out, leaving the room in impenetrable darkness.

CHAPTER IV

The difference between light and the lack of it is the difference between freedom and captivity, and the real reason that we pity a blind man is because he is a prisoner. This is true under normal conditions. Add to darkness dread of the supernatural, and the inevitable sum is panic.

Till that moment I doubt if Roberta or I had believed the black hand which touched her to be of other than natural origin. Ingrained thought-habit had accused Moore of trickery, even while it condemned the trick as unpleasant.

That was while the light burned. One instant later we were trapped prisoners of the dark, and instincts centuries old flung off thought-habit like a tissue cloak.

What had been a quiet, modern room became, in that instant, the devil-haunted jungle of forebears infinitely remote.

And it didn't help matters that just then "Horace" elected to be heard again. Alicia visible, Horace had seemed a vocal feat on her part. Alicia unseen, Horace became a discarnate fiend. That he was a fiend, vulgar and incongruous, only made his fiendishness more intolerable.

"How's this for a joke?" he inquired sardonically, "I never did like that lamp! Let's give it away, Jimmy. Tell your young fool friend to take the lamp away with him."

Soundlessly, without warning, something hard and slightly warm touched my cheek. I struck out wildly. My fist crashed through glass, there was a great smash and clatter from the floor, and mingled with it shout upon shout of fairly maniacal mirth. Then Moore's voice, cool but irritated:

"You'll have to stop these tricks, Horace. I'm ashamed of you! Breaking a valuable lamp like that. Our guests will believe you a common spirit or poltergeist."

"Moore, if you don't throw on the lights, I'll kill you for this!"

My own voice shook with mingled rage and dread. Of course, it might be he who had brought the lamp and held it against my face, but the very senselessness of the trick made it terrible in a queer, unhuman way.

"Stand still!" he commanded sharply. "Barbour, Miss Whitingfield, you are not children! Nothing will harm you, if you keep quiet. It was your own yielding to anger and fear that brought this crude force into play. Did it actually hit you with the lamp, Barbour?"

"I hit the lamp, but—"

"Exactly! Now keep quiet. Horace, may I turn on the lights?"

"If you do, you'll be sorry, Jimmy! Call me poltergeist or plain Dutch, there's somebody worse than me here tonight."

"What do you mean, Horace?"

"Oh, somebody that came along in with your scared young friends. He's a Joker, too, but I don't like him. He wants to get through the gates altogether, and stay through. If he does, a lot of people will be sorry: You say I'm rough, but say, Jimmy, this fellow is worse than rough. He's smooth! Get me? Too smooth. I'm keeping him back, and you know I'm stronger in the dark."

"Very well." I heard Moore laugh amusedly. His quiet matter-of-courseness should have deleted all terror from the affair. He was carrying on a conversation with a rather silly, rather vulgar man, of whom he was not afraid, but whose vagaries he indulged for reasons of expediency. That was the sound of it.

But the sense of it—there in the blackness—was such an indescribable horror to me as I cannot convey by words. There was more to this feeling than fear of Horace. I learned what nerves meant that night. If mine had all been on the outside of my skin, crawling, expectant of shock, I could have suffered no more keenly. Coward? Wait to judge that till you learn what the uncomprehending expectancy meant for me.

"Very well," laughed Moore. "But don't break any more lamps, Horace—please! Have some consideration for my pocketbook."

"Money! We haven't any pants-pockets my side of the line," Horace chuckled. "If I'm to keep the smooth fellow back, you must let me use my strength. Let me have my fun, Jimmy! What's a lamp or so between pals? And just to keep things interesting, suppose we bring out the big fellow in the closet?"

I heard a thud from the direction of the cabinet, a low chuckle, and then a huge panting sound. It sounded like an enormous animal. We had a sense of something living and enormous that had suddenly come out of nothing into the room.

"The hand!" screamed Roberta sharply. "It's the black-hand thing!"

I was hideously afraid that she was right. With her own clutching little hands on my arm, I sprang, dragging her with me. I didn't spring for where I thought Moore was, nor for where I supposed the door might be. There were only two thoughts in my head. One of a monstrous and wholly imaginary black giant; the other, a passionate desire for light.

By pure chance I brought up against the wall just beside a brass plate inset with two magical, blessed buttons. My fingers found them. Got the wrong button—the right one.

Flash! And we were out of demon-land and in a commonplace room again.

Not quite commonplace, though. True, no black, impossible giant inhabited it. The vast panting sound hand passed and though the lamp lay among the splinters of its wrecked shade and my hand was bleeding, a broken lamp and cut hand are possible incidentals of the ordinary.

But that woman in the chair was not!

Writhing, shrieking, foaming creatures like that have their place in a hospital—or a sick man's delirium—but not rightfully in an evening's entertainment for two unexpectant young people. Bert took one look and buried her face against my vest in an ecstasy of fear.

Moore was beside his wife, swiftly unclasping the steel manacles that held her, but finding time for a glaring side glance at me which expressed white-hot and concentrated rage.

I didn't understand. Alicia's previous spasms or seizures, though less violent than this, had been bad enough. Why should Moore eye me like that, when if anyone had a right to be furious it was I?

"The lights!" moaned Bert against my vest. "You turned on the lights, and it hurt her. I've read that somewhere—Oh, Clay, why don't you do something to help her and make her stop that horrible screaming?"

Moore heard and turned again, snarling. "You get out of here, Barbour! You've done harm enough!"

"Shan't I—shan't we call a doctor?" I stammered.

He didn't answer. Released, Alicia had subsided limply, a black heap in the chair, face on knees. The gurgling shrieks had lowered to a series of long, agonizing moans. I thought she was dying, and in a confused way felt that both Roberta and Moore blamed me.

The moans, too, had ceased. Was she dead?

Now Moore was trying to lift his wife out of the chair—and failing, for some reason. Instinctively I pushed Roberta aside and moved to help him.

And then, at last, that happened for which all the rest had been a prelude—for which, my whole life had been a prelude, as I was to learn one day. There came—how can I phrase it?

It was not a darkness, for I saw. It was not a vacuum, for most certainly I—everyone of us—continued to breathe. It was like—you know what happens sometimes in a thunderstorm? There is a hushed moment, when it is as if a mighty, invisible being had drawn in its breath—not breath of air, but of force. If you live in the suburbs and have alternating current, the lights go out—as if the current had been sucked back.

Static has the upper band of kinetic. A moment, and kinetic will rebel in a blinding, crashing river of fire from sky to earth. But till then, between earth and clouds there is a tension so terrific that it gives the awful sense of a void.

That happened in the room where we stood, though the force involved was not the physical one of electricity. There was the hushed moment, the sense of awful tension—of void—of strength sucked back like the current—

Without knowing how, I became aware that all the life in the room was suddenly, dreadfully centralizing around one of us. That one was Alicia.

I saw Moore move back from her. He had gone ghastly pale, and he waved his hands queerly. The straining sense of void which was also centralization increased. A numbness crept over me.

The invisible had drawn in its breath of pure force, and my life was undoubtedly a part of it.

There came a stirring of the black heap in the chair. Inexplicably, I felt as well as saw it. As if, standing by the wall, I was also in the chair. Roberta shivered. She was out of my sight, standing slightly behind me, but I felt that, too. No two of us were in physical contact, and yet some strange interfusion of consciousness was linking us more closely than the physical.

Again Alicia stirred. She cried out inarticulately. The centralization was around her, but not by her will. I felt a surge of resentment that was not mine, but Alicia's. Then I knew that there were more than four of us present, in the room. A fifth was here—invisible, strong, unifying the strength of us all for its own purpose—for a leap across the intangible barriers and into the living world.

Numbness was on me, cold dread, and a sense of some danger peculiarly personal to myself. It was coming now—now—

With another cry, Alicia shot suddenly erect. Her arms went out in a wide sweep that seemed to be struggling in an attempt to push something from her.

"!" she cried, and: "You! Back! Go back—go back—go back! Oh, you, Serapion!"

When kinetic revolts against static, blinding fire results. The tension in that room let go as suddenly as the lightning stroke, though I was the only one to feel it fully.

My body reeled against the wall. My spirit—I—the ego—reeled with it—beyond it—down—down—into darkness absolute—and into a nullity deeper than darkness' self.

Speed. In outer space there is room for it, and necessity. Between our sun and the nearest star where one may grow warm again there is space that a light ray needs centuries to cross.

The cold is cruel, and a wind blows there more biting than the winds of earth. Little, cold stars rush by like far-separated lamps on a country road, and double meteors, twin blazing eyes, swing down through the long black reaches. It is hard to avoid these, when they sweep so close, and one's hands are numb on the steering-wheel.

But one can't slow for that—nor even for a frightened voice at one's elbow, pleading, protesting, begging for the slowness that will let the cold overtake and annihilate us. "The cold!" I shouted against the wind. "Cold!"

"Well, if you're cold," wailed the harassed voice, "why don't you slow down? Clay! Clayton Barbour! I'll never ride again in a car with you, Clayton, if you don't slow down!"

Another pair of twin meteors rushed curving toward us. We avoided them, kept our course by the fraction of a safe margin, and as we did so the limitless vistas of interstellar space seemed to close in sharply and solidify.

Infinite shrank to finite with the jolt of a collision—and it was almost a real one. I swung to the left and barely avoided the tail of a farmer's wagon, ambling sedately along the road ahead of us. Then I not only slowed, but stopped, while the wagon creaked prosaically by. I sat at the wheel of a car—my own car—and that was Roberta Whitingfeld beside me.

"Sixty miles an hour!" she was saying indignantly. "You haven't touched the horn once, and you are sitting so that I can't get at it."

I said nothing. Desperately I was trying to adjust the unadjustable.

This road was real. The numbness and chill were passing, and the air of a summer night blew warm on my cheek. That wild rush of the spirit through space was already fading into place as a dream memory.

But there had been some kind of an hiatus in realities. My last definite memory was of—Alicia Moore. Alicia—upright—rebellious—crying out a name.

"Clay!" A note of concern had replaced Roberta's indignation. "Why do you sit there so still? Answer me! Are you ill? What is the matter?"

"Nothing."

That was a lie, of course, but instinctive as self-protection. I must get straight somehow, but I wouldn't confide the need even to Roberta. In the most ordinary tone I apologized for my reckless driving and started the car again. We were on a familiar road, outside the city, but one that would take us by roundabout ways to our home in the suburbs.

I drove slowly, for it was very necessary that Roberta should talk. By listening I might be able to get straight without betraying myself, and indeed, before we reached home, I had a fairly clear idea of what had happened in the blank interim.

A first wild surmise that the Moore episode had been a dream in its entirety was banished almost at once. As nearly as I could gather, without direct questioning, from the time when I reeled back against the wall until my return to self-consciousness some sixty minutes later, I had behaved so normally in outward appearance that not even Roberta had seen a difference.

My body had evidently not fallen to the floor, nor showed any signs of fainting or unconsciousness. Alicia seemed to have returned to her senses at the same time that I lost mine, for Roberta spoke of her hostess' quiet air of indifference that amounted almost to scorn for the concern that we—Bert and I, mind you!—expressed for her.

Moore, for his part, it seemed, had recovered his temper and been rather apologetic and anxious that I, at least, should repeat my visit. I had been noncommittal on the subject—for which Roberta now commended me—and then we had come away together.

After that, the hallucination I had suffered, of myself as a disembodied entity, careering from one planetary system to another, had synchronized with an actual career in the car where road-lamps simulated stars and occasional cars traveling in the opposite direction provided the stimuli for my dream-meteors.

A man hypnotized might have done what I did, and as successfully. To myself, then, I said that I had been hypnotized. That in a manner yet to be explained either Moore or his wife had hypnotized me and allowed me to leave their house under that influence. I tried to determine what reckoning I should have with them later. But it was a failure. I was frankly scared.

An hour had been jerked bodily, out of my conscious life. If, in the ordinary and orthodox manner, I had lain insensible through that hour, it wouldn't have mattered so much. Instead of that, an 'I' that was not I appeared to have taken charge of my affairs and in such a manner that a person very near and dear to me had perceived nothing wrong. It was that which frightened me.

The last traces of daze, and shock released my mind, the instinct to keep its lapse a secret only grew stronger. Fortunately I found concealment easy. Speeding was not so far from my occasional habit that Roberta had thought much of that part of the episode. Her vigorous protests had been largely on account of my failure to use the horn.

Dropping the subject with her usual quick good-nature, she talked of our remarkable first experience with a "real medium," and disclosed the fact—not surprising perhaps—that she had been considerably less impressed than I. In retrospect she blamed her own nerves for most of the excitement.

"I may be unfair, Clay," she confided, "but truly, I can't help believing that Mrs. Moore is just a clever, hysterical woman who has deluded poor Mr. Moore into a faith in 'spirit voices.'"

"The black hand? The little flames?"

"Did we really see them? Don't you think the woman may have some kind of hypnotic power, like—oh, like the mango trick that everybody's heard they do in India? You know. A tree grows right up out of the ground while you watch; but it doesn't really, of course. You're hypnotized, and only think you see it. Couldn't everything we saw and heard tonight have been a—a kind of hypnotic trick? And—now, with all the screaming and fuss she had made, Mrs. Moore was so calm and cool when we left! I think it was all put on, and the rest was hypnotism."

"You're a very clever little girl, Berty," I commented, and meant it. If there was one thing I wished to believe, it was that Alicia Moore had faked.

We knew nearly as little about hypnotism as we did of psychic phenomena, real or so-called. But the word had a good sound to me. I had been hypnotized. Hypnotized! That Fifth Presence in the room had existed only in my own overborne imagination. The whole affair was—

"Berty," I said, "we've been through a highly unpleasant experience, and it's my fault. Nils warned me against those people, but I was stubborn mule enough to believe I wished to know more of them. I don't, and we don't—you and I. The truth is, Berty, I feel pretty foolish over the whole business. Had no right to take you to such a place. Downright dangerous—queer, irresponsible people like that! Say, do you mind not telling Cathy, for instance?"

"If you won't tell mother!"

She giggled. I could picture myself relating that weird and unconventional tale to the stately Mrs. Whitingfield! Up went my right hand.

"Hear me swear! I, Clayton S. Barbour, do solemnly vow silence—"

"Full name, or it isn't legal!" trilled the girl beside me.

"Oh, very well! I, Clayton Barbour, do—"

I stopped with a tightening of the throat. As the word "" passed my lips, the Fifth Presence had shut down close about me.

Out of space-time—wrapped away in cloudy envelopes of oblivion-

"Clayton!" A clear young voice out of the clouds. They shriveled to nothing, and I was loosed to my world again. "Why, Clayton!" repeated Roberta. "How did that woman know your middle name?"

My right hand dropped to the wheel, and the car leaped forward.

"Did you tell her?" insisted Roberta.

"No," I answered shortly. "Berquist told Moore, I supposed. How do I know?"

"Someone must have told her," Bert agreed. "It isn't as if it were an ordinary name that she might have hit on by guessing."

"Oh, it isn't so unusual. There have been Sera—there; have been men of that name in my mother's family for generations. I was given the name in remembrance of my mother's brother. He died only a few months before I was born, and she had cared a lot for him. But don't let's talk of the name any more. I always hated it. Sounds silly, like a girl's name—I—I—Oh, forget the name! Here we are at home, and there's your mother in the window looking for us."

"We're awfully late!"

"Tell her the Moores were very interesting people," I suggested grimly.

That night, though I slept, Alicia Moore and the Fifth Presence—in various unpleasant shapes—haunted me through some exceedingly restless hours.

CHAPTER V

That a man may retire to his bed unknown and wake up famous is a truism of long standing. There is a parallel truth not half so pleasant. A man—a whole family—may retire wealthy and wake up paupers.

My father was the practically inactive senior member of his firm, and the reins had so far left his hands that when the blow fell it was hard for him to get a grasp on the situation or even credit it.

Rather shockingly, the first word we had of disaster came through the morning paper in a blare-headed column announcing the suicide of Frederic Hutchinson. Suicide without attempt at concealment. A scrubwoman, entering the private offices of Barbour & Hutchinson early that morning, had fairly trodden in the junior partner's scattered brains.

There followed a week of torment—of sordid revelations of unwise speculation, and ever increasing despair. A week that left dad a shaken, tremulous old man, and the firm of Barbour & Hutchinson, grain brokers, an unpleasant problem to be dealt with by the receivers.

Dad had known his partner for a clever man, and no doubt he was formerly a trustable one. But when the disease called speculation takes late root, its run is likely to be more virulent than in a younger victim. All Hutchinson's personal estate had been absorbed. His family were left in worse predicament than ours—or would have been, save that dad's peculiar sense of honor caused him to throw every cent he owned, independent of the firm, into the pit where that firm's honor had vanished, in an attempt to save it.

Unfortunately he possessed not nearly enough to satisfy the creditors and re-establish the business. As my mother pointed out, the disgrace that had been all Fred Hutchinson's was now dad's for impoverishing his family when, under the terms of partnership and the law of our State, most of his personal investments and realty could have been held free from liability.

And to that dad had only one, and to my mind somewhat appalling, reply:

"Let Clay go to work in earnest, then. Perhaps some day my son will clear the slate of what scores I've failed to settle!"

Well, great God, can a young fellow carefully trained to have everything he wants without trying turn financial genius in a week?

If it hadn't been for Roberta, I think I should have thrown up the sponge and fairly run away from it all. Her faith, though, stirred a chord of ambition that those of my own blood failed to touch, and her stately Charlestonian mother emerged from stateliness into surprising sympathy.

Then Dick Vansittart, the unregenerate youngster who had been my dearest pal in college days, got me a job with the Colossus Trust Company, the bank of which his father was president and where he himself loafed about intermittently.

Even I knew that the salary offered was more commensurate with our needs than with what I was worth. Vansittart, Sr., a gruff old lion of a man, growled at me through a personal interview which ended in: "You won't earn your salt for six months, Barbour, but maybe Terne can put up with you. Try it, anyway!"

Terne was the second vice-president, whose assistant, or secretary, or general errand-boy, it was proposed that I become. I reached for my hat.

"Sorry to have bothered you, Mr. Vansittart! I would hardly care to receive pay except on the basis that it was earned."

The lion roared.

"Sit down! Don't you try Dick's high mannerisms with me! If I can tolerate Dick in this bank, I can tolerate you; but there's going to be one difference. You'll play the man and work till you do earn your wages, or you'll go out! Understand?"

"I merely meant—"

"Never mind that." The savage countenance before me softened to a leonine benevolence. "Clayton Barbour's son wants no charity, but, you young fool, don't I know that? Your father has, swamped himself to pay debts that weren't his. Now I choose to pay a debt that isn't mine, but Dick's!"

I must have looked my bewilderment.

"I mean," he thundered, "that when my son was expelled from the college he disgraced he nearly took you with him! You cubs believe you carry your shame on your own shoulders. You never think of us. I've crossed the street three times to avoid meeting your father! Earn your wages here, so that I can shake hands with him next time. Here—take this note to Mr. Terne. His office is next the cashier's. Go to work!"

I went, but outside the door found Van waiting for me, smiling ironically.

"You heard?" I muttered.

"Not being stone deaf, yes. The governor doesn't mind publicity where I'm concerned, eh? Interested passersby in the street might hear, for all he cares. Oh, well—truth is mighty and must prevail. Wish you luck, Clay, and there's Fatty Terne coming now. So long!"

I was left to present my note to a dignified person who had just emerged from the Cashier's office. "Fatty" was a merciless nickname for him, and unfair besides. The second vice-president's large figure suggested strength rather than overindulgence. Beneath his dignity he proved a kindly, not domineering man, much overworked himself, but patient with early mistakes from a new helper.

He shared one stenographer with another official, and seemed actually grateful when I offered to learn shorthand during spare hours in order to be of more use with the correspondence. I was quite infected with the work fever for a while, and saw little of Van, who let me severely alone from the first day I entered the bank.

His new standoffishness didn't please me exactly, but I was too busy to think much of him one way or the other. At home, however, things went not so well. Since the house had been sold over our heads, we were forced into painfully small quarters. There was a little place near-by that belonged to my mother. It had stood empty for a year, and though not much better than a cottage, her ownership of it solved the rent problem, and, as she bitterly explained, we no longer needed servants' rooms nor space for the entertainment of guests.

Mother and Cathy undertook the housework, while dad fooled about with paint-pots and the like, trying to delude himself into the belief that paint, varnish, and a few new shelves here and there would make a real home for us out of this wretched shack; for that is what Cathy and I called it privately.

All the problems of home life had taken on new, ugly, uncomfortable angles, and I spent as little time among them as I decently could.

Roberta had no more complaints to make of "sixty miles an hour and never touched the horn." My car had gone with the rest. We went on sedate little walks, like a country pair, tried to prefer movies to grand opera, and piled up heart-breaking dream-castles for consolation.

Two months slid by, and in that while our adventure at the "dead-alive house," as Roberta had named Moore's place, was hardly mentioned between us. Once or twice, indeed, she referred to it, but there was for me an oppressive distastefulness in the subject that made me lead our conversations elsewhere.

On the very heels of the catastrophic passing of my father's firm I had received a brief note from Moore. He expressed concern and sympathy, adding in the same breath, as it were, that he hoped I had been well enough interested the other evening to wish to walk farther along the path of Psychical research.

I regarded his concern as impertinent and his hope as impudent, considering my unpleasant memories of the first visit. I tore the letter up without answering it. After that I heard no more from him, and it was not until the second month's ending that a thing occurred which forced the whole matter vividly upon my recollection.

"If dear had not been taken from us," said my mother, "we should be living in a civilized manner, and my children and I would not have been driven to manual labor!"

Dad kept his eyes on his plate, refraining from answer. He had been guilty of an ill-advised criticism on Cathy's cooking, and, from that, discussion had run through all the ramifications of domestic misery until I was tempted to leave dinner unfinished and escape to my usual refuge, the Whitingfields.

But the mention of my uncle's name had a peculiar effect on me. A slight swimming sensation behind the eyes, a gripping tightness at the back of my neck—!

The feeling passed, but left me trembling so that I remained in my place, fearing to rise lest I betray myself. As before, some deep-seated instinct fought that. The weakness was like a shameful wound, to be at all costs hidden.

"Had he lived," continued my mother, "he would have seen to it that we weren't brought to this. No one near poor was ever allowed to be uncomfortable!"

Dad's eyes flashed up with a glint of spirit that he had never before showed in this connection.

"Is that so? I know he kept remarkably comfortable himself, but I can't recall his feathering anyone's nest but his own."

"Don't slander the dead!" came her sharp retort. "Why, you owe the very house over your head to him! And if it hadn't been that his thoughtfulness left it in my name you wouldn't have that. You would have robbed your children and me of even this pitiful shelter—"

"Evelyn—please!"

"It's true! And then you dare cast slurs and innuendoes at poor—"

"I gave him the house in the first place," dad muttered.

She rose, eyes flashing and filled with tears. "Yes, you did! And this shameful little hole was all he had to live in—and die in! was a saint!" she declared. "A saint! He was—he was universally loved!"

And with that, my mother swept from the room. Cathy followed, though with a sneaking glance of sympathy for dad. Tempestuous exits on mother's part had been frequent as far back as I could remember, and as they were invariably followed by hours in which someone must sit with her and the house must be kept dead silent, we other three had the fellow-feeling of victims.

Dad eyed me across the table. "Son," he said, "what is your middle name?"

"Ser-Ser-Samuel!" I ended desperately. My heart, for no obvious reason, had begun a palpitation. Why couldn't they let that name alone?

He looked surprised, and then laughed. "You are right, son. I was about to give you warning—to forbid your becoming such a saint as your esteemed namesake. But I guess that isn't needed. The Samuels of the world stand on their own feet, as you do now, thank Heaven! A Samuel for the in you, then, and never forget it!"

He could not guess the frantic struggle going on beneath my calm exterior. There is, I believe, a psychopathic condition in which sound-waves produce visual sensations; a musical note, for example, being seen as a blob of scarlet, or the sustained blast of a bugle as a ribbony, orange-colored streak. Some such confusion of the senses seemed to have occurred in me, only in my case one single sound produced it, and the result was not color but a feeling of pressure, dizziness, suffocation.

Fighting for control, I knew that another iteration of the sound in question would cost me the battle. Dad's mouth opened, and simultaneously I rose. Opinions on my uncle's character, pro or con, didn't interest me half so much as the problem of excusing myself in a steady voice, walking from table to doorway without a stagger, and finally escaping from that room before the fatal name could be spoken again.

These feats accomplished, I managed to get up the stairs and into my own room, where I locked the door and dropped, face downward, across the bed. Though the evening was cool, my whole body was drenched with sweat and my brain reeled sickeningly.

One may get help from queer sources. Van, in our gay junior year—his last at college—had initiated me into a device for keeping steady when the last drink has been one too many. You mentally recite a poem or speech or the multiplication table—any old thing will do. Fixing the mind in that way seems to soothe the gyrating interior and enables a fellow at least to fall asleep like a gentleman.

In my present distress that came back to me. Still fighting off the unknown with one-half of my mind, I scrabbled around in the other half for some definite memorization to take hold of.

There was none. The very multiplication table swam a jumble of numbers. Then I caught a rhyme beginning in the back of my head, and fixed my attention on it feverishly. Over and over the words said themselves, first haltingly, then with increasing certainty. It was a simple, jingling little prayer that every child in the English-speaking world, I suppose, has learned past forgetfulness. "Now I lay me down to Sleep—"

Again—again—by the tenth repetition of "I pray the Lord my soul to take," I had wrenched my mind away from—that other—and had its whole attention on the rhyme. At last, following a paroxysm of trembling, I knew myself the victor. Once more the Fifth Presence had released me.

Panting and weak from reaction, I sat up. What ailed me? How, in reason and common sense, could the sound of any man's name have this effect on me?

Hypnotism? Nearly two months had elapsed since my first trouble of this kind, and without recurrence in the interim. No, and come to think of it, I couldn't recall having heard the name spoken in that while, either. ! It was only when uttered aloud that the word had power over me. I could think of it without any evil effect. And that name on Alicia's lips had been my last vivid impression before I lost self-consciousness and walked out of, Moore's house, an intelligent automaton for sixty minutes after.

Scraps of psychology came back to me. Hypnotism—hypnotic suggestion. Could a man be shocked into hypnotic sleep, awaken, and weeks later be swayed by a sound that had accompanied the first lapse?

One way, I set myself very firmly. In cool judgment I was no believer in ghosts. The very thought brought a smile to my lips. My uncle had died before I was born; but, though dad had for some reason disliked him, by all accounts my namesake had been a genial, easy-going, agreeable gentleman, rather characterless, perhaps, and inclined to let the other fellow work, but not a man whose spirit could be imagined as a half-way efficient "haunt."

! No, and neither would he probably have flung away his own and his family's comfort for a point of fine-drawn honor. Was dad in the right? I had tried to reserve criticism there, and in action I had certainly backed him to the limit. Inevitably, though from yet far-off, I could see the loss of Roberta grinding down upon me. She couldn't wait my convenience forever, you know. Some other fellow-some free, unburdened chap—

I buried my head in my hands.

Then I dropped them and sprang erect, every nerve alert.

I had closed my eyes, and in that instant, a face had leaped into being behind their shut lids. The face was not Roberta's, though I had been thinking of her. Moreover, it had lacked any dreamlike quality. It had come real—real as if the man had entered my bedroom and thrust his face close to mine.

As my eyes flicked open, it had vanished, leaving me quivering with a strange resentment—an anger, as if some intimate privacy had been invaded. I stood with clenched fists, more angry than amazed at first, but not daring to shut my eyes lest it return.

What had there been about the queer vision that was so loathsome?

The face of a man around forty years it had seemed, smooth-shaven, boyish in a manner, with a little inward twist at the mouth corners, an amused slyness to the clear, light-blue eyes, The face of an easygoing, take-life's-jokes-as-they-come sort of fellow, amiable, pleasant, and, in some indefinite fashion—horrible.

I was sure I had never seen the man in real life, though there had been a vague familiarity about him, too.

About him! A dream—a vision.

"Clayton Barbour," I muttered through shut teeth, "if it has reached the point where a word throws you into spasm and you are afraid to close your eyes, you'd better consult a doctor; and that is exactly what I shall do!"

CHAPTER VI

Nils Berquist has his own ways, and whether or not they were practical or customary to mankind at large influenced him in no degree. He called himself a socialist, but in pure fact he was simply one of those persons who require a cause to fight for and argue about, as a Hedonist craves his pleasures, or the average man an income.

Real socialism, with the communal interests it implies, was foreign to Berquist's very nature. He could get along, in a withdrawn kind of way, with almost anyone. He would share what small possessions he had with literally anyone. But his interest went to such abstractions of thought as were talked and written by men of his own kind, while himself—his mind—he kept for the very few. Those are the qualities of an aristocrat, not a socialist.

One result of his paradoxical attitude showed in the fact that when it came to current news, Nils was as ignorant a man as you could meet in a day's walk. My various troubles and activities had kept me from thinking of him, but when I again happened on Nils in town one evening it hurt my feelings to discover that the spectacular downfall of Barbour & Hutchinson might have occurred on another planet, so far as he was concerned.

News that had been blazoned in every paper was news to him all this time afterward. Even learning it from me in person, he said little, though this silence might have been caused by embarrassment. Roberta was with me, and to tie Nils' tongue you had only to lead him into the presence of femininity in the person of a young, pretty girl.

I at last recalled the fact, and because for a certain reason I wished a chance to talk with him where he would talk, I asked if he couldn't run out some night and have dinner with us. Cathy's cooking was nothing wonderful, but I knew Nils wouldn't mind that, nor the cramped quarters we had to live in. I reckoned on taking him up to my own room later for a private confab.

After a short hesitation he accepted.

"You take care of yourself, Clay," he added. "You're looking pale—run down. Don't tell me you've been laid up sick along with all this other trouble?"

"No, indeed, old man. Working rather harder than I used to and—lately I haven't slept very well. Bad dreams—but aside from that, nothing serious."

After a few more words, we parted, he striding off on his lonely way to some bourne unknown; Roberta and I proceeding toward the movies.

A fortnight had passed since the strange face had made its first appearance. If Nils thought I looked pale, there was reason for it. "Bad dreams," I had told him, but bad dreams were less than all.

My resolve to visit a doctor had come to nothing. I had called, indeed, upon our family physician, as I had meant. The moment I entered his presence, however, that instinct for concealment which had prevented me from confiding in Roberta or my family rose up full strength. The symptoms I actually laid before Dr. Lloyd produced a smile and a prescription that might as well have been the traditional bread pills. I didn't bother to have it filled. I went out as alone with my secret as when I entered.

A face—boyish in manner, pleasant, half-smiling usually; with an amused slyness to the clear, light-blue eyes; an agreeable inward quirk at the corners of the finely cut lips. I had come to know every lineament ultimately well.

It had not returned again until some time after the first appearance. Then—at the bank, the afternoon following my futile conference with Dr. Lloyd—I happened to close my eyes, and it was there, behind the lids.

There was a table in Mr. Terne's office, over which he used to spread out his correspondence and papers. I was seated at one side of the table and he on the other, and I started so violently that he dropped his pen and made a straggling ink-feather across the schedule of securities he was verifying.

He patiently blotted it, and I made such a fuss over getting out the ink-eradicator and restoring the sheet of minutely figured ledger paper to neatness, that he forgot to ask what had made me jump in the first place.

After that the face was with me so often that if I shut my eyes and saw nothing, its absence bothered me. I would feel then that the face had got behind me, perhaps, and acquired the bad habit of casting furtive glances over my shoulder.

You may think that if one must be burdened with a companion invisible to the world, such a good-humored countenance as I have described would be the least disagreeable. But that was not so.

There was to me a subtle hatefulness about it—like a thing beautiful and at the same time vile, which one hates in fear of coming to love it.

I never called the face "him," never thought of it as a man, nor gave it a man's name. I was afraid to! As if recognition would lend the vision power, I called it the Fifth Presence, and hated it.

As days of this passed, there came a time when the face began trying to talk to me. There, at least, I had the advantage. Though I could see the lips move, forming words, by merely opening my eyes I was able to banish it, and so avoid learning what it wished to say.

In bed, I used to lie with my eyes wide open sometimes, for hours, waiting for sleep to come suddenly. When that happened I was safe, for though my dreams were often bad, the face never invaded them.

I discovered, too, that the name had in a measure lost power to throw me off balance, since the face had come. My mother continued to harp on the superiority of my dead uncle's character, and how he would have shielded us from the evils that had befallen, until dad acquiesced in sheer self-protection. But though I didn't like to hear her talk of him, and though the sound of the name invariably quickened my heartbeat, hearing neither increased nor diminished the vision's vividness.

It was with me, however, through most of my waking hours—waiting behind my lids—and if I looked pale, as Nils said, the wonder is that I was able to appear at all as usual. So I wished to talk with Nils, hoping that to the man who had warned me against the Moores, I could force myself to confide the distressing aftermath of my visit at the "dead-alive house."

He had promised to come out the next night but one, which was Wednesday. Unfortunately, however, I missed seeing him then, after all, and because of an incident whose climax was to give the Fifth Presence a new and unexpected significance.

About two-thirty Wednesday afternoon I ran up the steps of the Colossus Trust, and at the top collided squarely with Van, Jr. By the slight reel with which he staggered against a pillar and caught hold of it, I knew that Van had been hitting the high spots again and hoped he had not been interviewing his father in that condition. On recovering his balance, Van stood up steady enough.

"Old scout Clay! Say, you look like a pale, pallid, piffling freshwater clam, you do. 'Pon my word, I'm ashamed of the old Colossus. The old brass idol has sucked all the blood out of you. My fault, serving up the best friend I ever had as a—a helpless sacrifice to my father's old brass Colossus. Come on with me—you been good too long!"

He playfully pretended to tear off the brass-lettered name of the trust company, which adorned the wall beside him, cast it down and trample on it. When I tried to pass he caught my arm. "Come on!"

"Can't," I explained quietly. "Mr. Terne was the best man at a wedding today, but he left me a stack of work."

Van sniffed. "Hub! I know that wedding. I was invited to that wedding, but I wouldn't go. Measly old teetotaler wedding! Just suits Fatty Terne. When you get married, Clay, I'll send along about eleven magnums for a wedding present, and then I'll come to your wedding!"

"You may—when it happens." Again I tried to pass him.

"Wait a minute. You poor, pallid work slave—you know what I'm going to do for you?"

"Get me fired, by present prospects. I must—"

"You must not. Just listen. You know Barney Finn"'

"Not personally. Let me go now, Van and I'll see you later."

"Barney Finn," he persisted doggedly, "has got just the biggest li'l engine that ever slid round a track. Now you wait a minute. Barney's another friend of mine. Told me all about it. Showed it to me. Showed me how it's going to make every other wagon at Fairview tomorrow look like a hand-pushed per-perambulator!"

"All right. Come around after the race and tell me how Finn made out. Please—"

"Wait. You're my friend, Clay, and I like you. You put a thousand bones on Finney's car, and say goodbye to old Colossus."

I laughed. But he went on.

"My dear friend, you misjudge me, sadly—yes, indeed! Didn't I wrest one pitiful Century from Colossus five minutes ago, and isn't that the last that stood between me and starvation, and ain't I going right out and plaster that century on Finn's car? Would I im—impoverish the Colossus and me, puttin' that last century on anything but a sure win? Come across, boy!"

Now, one might think that Van's invitation lacked attractiveness to a sober man. I happened to know, however, that drunk or sober, his judgment was good on one subject, the same being motorcars. Barney Finn, moreover, was a speed-track veteran with a mighty reputation at his back. He had, in the previous year, met several defeats, due to bad luck, in my opinion, but they had brought up the odds. If he had something particularly good and new in his car for tomorrow's race at Fairview, there was a chance for somebody to make a killing, as Van said. "What odds?" I queried.

"For each li'l bone you plant, twelve li'l bones will blossom. Good enough? I could get better, but this will be off Jackie Rosenblatt, an' you know that he's a reg'lar old Colossus his own self. Solid an' square. Hock his old high silk hat before he'd welch."

"Yes, Rosie's square." I did some quick mental figurine, and then pulled a thin sheaf of bills from an inner coat pocket. Instantly, Van had snatched them out of my hand.

"Not all!" I exclaimed sharply. "Take fifty, but I brought that to deposit—"

"Deposit it with Jackie! Why, you old miser with your bank account! Four entire centuries, and you weepin' over poverty! Say, Clay, how much is twelve times four?"

"Forty-eight, but—"

"Lightnin' calculator!" he admired. "Say, doesn't forty-eight hundred make a bigger noise in your delikite ear than four measly centuries? Come across!"

I don't think I nodded. I am almost sure that I had begun reaching my hand to take all, or most of those bills back. But Van thought otherwise. "Right, boy!"

With plunging abruptness he was off down the steps. I hesitated. Forty-four hundred. Then I caught myself and was after him, but too late. His speedy gray roadster was already nosing recklessly into the traffic. Before I reached the bottom step it had shot around the corner and was gone.

Off Mr. Terne's spacious office there was a little glass-enclosed, six-by-eight cubbyhole which I called my own.

Ten o'clock Thursday morning found me seated in the one chair, staring at a pile of canceled notes on the desk before me. I had started to check them half an hour ago, but so far just one checkmark showed on the list beside them. I had something worse to think of than canceled notes.

As I sat, I could hear Mr. Terne fussing about the outer office. Then I heard him go out. About two minutes afterward the door banged open so forcibly that I half started up, conscience clamoring.

But it wasn't the second vice returning in a rage. It was Van. He fairly bolted into my cubbyhole, closed the door, pitched his hat in a corner, and swung himself to a seat on my desk-edge, scattering canceled notes right and left. There he sat, hands clasped, staring at me in a perfect stillness which contrasted dramatically with his violent entry. His eyes looked dark and sunken in a strained, white face. My nerves were inappreciative of drama.

"Where were you last night?" I demanded irritably. "I hunted for you around town till nearly midnight."

"What? Oh, I was way out in—I don't know exactly. Some dinky roadhouse. I pretty nearly missed the race and—and I wish to Heaven I had, Clay!" He passed a shaking hand across his eyes.

"Did Finn lose?" I snapped. "But—why, the race can hardly be more than started yet!"

"Finn started!" he gulped.

"Ditched?" I gasped, a flash of inspiration warning me of what was coming.

He nodded. "Turned turtle on the second lap and—say, boy—I helped dig him out and carry him off—you know, I liked Barney. It was—bad. The mechanism broke his back clean—flung against a post—but Barney—say, what was left of him kind of—kind of came apart—when we—" He stopped short, gulped again, and: "Guess I'm in bad shape this morning," he said huskily. "Nerves all shot to pieces."

I should have imagined they would be. A man straight from an all-night debauch can't witness a racing-car accident, help handle the human wreckage afterward, and go whistling merrily to tell his friends the tale.

I expressed that, though in more kindly chosen words, and then we both were silent a minute. Barney Finn had not been my friend, or even acquaintance, and while I was vicariously touched by Van's grief and horror, my own dilemma wasn't simplified by this news. Yet I hated to fling sordidness in the face of tragedy by speaking of money.

"Afterward I didn't feel like watching the race out." As Van spoke, I heard the outer door open again. This time it really was Mr. Terne, for I recognized his step.

"So I came straight here," Van continued.

My own door opened, and a kindly, dignified figure appeared there.

"Barbour," said the second vice, "have you that—ah, good morning, Richard." He nodded rather coldly to Van, and went on to ask me for the list I was supposed to be at work on.

When I explained that the checking wasn't quite finished, he turned away; then glanced back.

"By the way, Barbour," he said, "Prang dropped me a line saving that when you were in his office yesterday he paid up our hundred he has owed me since last June. If you were too late to deposit yesterday afternoon, get it from my box and we'll put it in with this check from the United."

I felt myself going fiery-red. "Sorry," I said. "I'll let you have that money this afternoon, Mr. Terne, I—I—"

"He gave it to me to deposit for him, and I used it for something else," broke in Van with the utmost coolness.

On occasion Van's brain worked with flashlight rapidity. He had put two and two of that four hundred together while another man might have been wondering about it. Terne stared, first at Van, then at me.

"You—you gave it—" he began slowly.

"He came here for your pass-book," ran Van's glib tongue. "I dropped in on him, and as I was going out past the tellers, I offered to put it in for him. Then I stuck it in my pocket, forgot it till too late, and needing some cash last night, I used that. Barbour has been throwing fits ever since I told him. I'll get it for you this afternoon."

Terne stared some more, and Van returned the look with cool insolence.

A brick-reddish color crept up the second v.p.'s cheeks, his mouth compressed to an unfamiliar straightness, and turning suddenly he walked out of not only my cubbyhole but his own office. The door shut with a rattle of jarred glazing.

"You shouldn't have done that!" I breathed.

"Oh, rats! Fatty Terne's gone to tell the old man. But he'll get thrown out. No news to the old man, about me, and he's sick of hearing it. Anyway, this is my fault, Clay' and I ought to stand the gaff. You've worked like the devil here, and then I come along and spoil everything. Drunken fool, me! Knew I'd queer you if we got together, and till yesterday I had sense enough to keep off. When I took those bills I knew there was something wrong, but I was too lit up to have any sense about it. Plain highway robbery! Never mind, old pal, I'll bring you back the loot this afternoon if I have to bust open one of the old Colossus' vaults for it!"

At my elbow the office phone jingled.

"Just a minute," I said. "No; wait, Van. Hello. Hel—Oh, Mr. Vansittart? Yes, sir. Be over at once, sir. Yes, he's here. What? Yes—" The other receiver had clicked up.

"We're in for it," I muttered. "Apparently your father hasn't thrown Terne out!"

Vansittart, Sr., the gruff old lion, granted lax discipline to no man under his control save one; and even Van, Jr., was, if not afraid, at least a bit wary of him. Though he had taken me on in the bank at a far higher wage than my services were worth, he had also made it very clear that so far as I was concerned, favoritism ended there. For me, I was sure the truth of the present affair would mean instant discharge.

"Shut the door!" he growled as we entered. "Now, Dick, I'll thank you to explain for exactly what reason you stole Mr. Terne's four hundred."

"Stole!" Van's slim figure stiffened and he went two shades whiter.

"Stole, yes! I said, stole. That is the usual term for appropriating money without the owner's consent."

"I don't accuse the boy of theft!" Terne's set face of anger relaxed suddenly. He didn't like Van, but he was a man who could not be unfair if he tried.

"Keep out of this, Terne—please. Dick, I'm waiting."

"Well, really," Van drawled "if you put it that way, I couldn't say what I did use the money for. There was a trifle of four hundred, owned, I believe, by Mr. Terne, which I borrowed, intending to return it in a few hours—"

"From what fund?" The old man was alert. I felt instinctively that this interview was a bit different from any that Van had been through heretofore. "Are you aware that your account in this bank is already overdrawn to the sum of—" he consulted a slip before him—"of forty-nine dollars and sixty cents? You perhaps have reserve funds at your command elsewhere?"

Van looked his father in the eye. What he saw must have been unusual. His brows went up slightly and the same fighting look came into his face which I had seen there when he and I confronted the faculty together. On that occasion I had been genuinely inclined to meekness. I remained in college while Van was thrown out.

He laughed lightly. "Excuse me half an hour while I run out and sell the li'l old roadster. Forty-nine sixty, you said? I'll pay you yours first, dad!"

"That's kind! After stealing one man's money you propose selling another man's car to replace it. Yes, my car, I said. What have you got in this world but your worthless brains and body to call your own? Wait. We'll go into this matter of ownership more deeply in a few minutes. Barbour," he whirled on me, "you allowed funds belonging to your supervisor to pass into unauthorized hands. That is not done in this bank. As things stand, I shall leave your case to Mr. Terne, but first you will make one direct' statement. I wish it made so that no question can arise afterward. Did you or did you not hand four hundred dollars in bills, the property of Mr. Terne, to my—to my son?"

It was up to me in earnest. I was now sure beyond doubt of what Van had run against. His parent had turned at last, and even the whole truth would barely suffice to save him. My lips opened. To blame though he was in a way, Van mustn't suffer seriously in my protection. I could not forget that momentary hesitation on my part, save for which I could easily have retrieved the bills before Van was out of reach.

"I gave it to him," I began.

And then, abruptly, silently, another face flashed in between me and the president. Instead of Vansittart's dark, angry eyes, I was staring into a pair of clear, amused, light-blue, ones. A finely cut mouth half smiled at me with lips that moved.

Always theretofore the face had come only when my lids were closed. Its wish to communicate with me—and that it did wish to communicate I was sure as if the thing had been a living man, following me about and perpetually tugging at my sleeve—had been a continual menace, but one which I had grown to feel secure from because the thing's power seemed so limited.

Now, with my eyes wide open, there hung the face in mid air. It was not in the least transparent. That is, its intervening presence obscured Vansittart's countenance as completely as though the head of a real man had thrust in between us. And yet—it is hard to express, but there was that about it, a kind of flatness, a lack of normal three-dimensional solidity, which gave it the look of a living portrait projected on the atmosphere.

I knew without even glancing toward them that Van and Mr. Terne did not see the thing as I did. It was there for me alone. At the moment, though I fought the belief again later, I knew beyond question that what I beheld was the projection of a powerful, external will, the same which, with Alicia's dynamic force to aid, had once actually taken possession of my body.

The finely cut, lips moved. No audible sound came from them, but as they formed words, the speech was heard in my brain distinctly as if conveyed by normal sound vibrations through the eardrums. It was silent sound. The tone was deep, rather agreeable, amiably amused:

"You have said enough," the face observed pleasantly. "You have told the truth; now stop there. Your friend has a father to deal with, while you have an employer. He is willing to shoulder all the blame, and for you to expose your share in it will be a preposterous folly. Remember, that hard as you have worked, you are receiving here twice the money you are worth—three times what you can hope to begin on elsewhere. Remember the miserable consequences of your own father's needless sacrifices. Remember how often, and very justly, you have wished that he had thought less of a point of fine-drawn honor, and more of his family's happiness. Will you commit like folly?"

I can't tell, so that anyone will understand, what a wave of accumulated memories and secret revolts against fate overswept me as I stared hard into the smiling, light-blue eyes. But I fought.

Grimly I began again. "I gave it to him..." and then—stopped.

"That's enough." This time it was Vansittart speaking. "You may go, Barbour. Mr. Terne, I will ask you to leave us. You will receive my personal check for the amount you have lost."

"But-but—" I stammered desperate while those clear eyes grew more amused more dominating.

The old man's hard-held calmness broke in a roar. "Get out! Both of you! Go!"

Mr. Terne laid his hand on my arm, and reluctantly I allowed myself to be steered toward the door. As I turned away the face did not float around with the turning of my eyes.

It hung in mid air, save for that odd, un-dimensional flatness real as any of the three other faces there. When my back was to the president, the—the Fifth Presence was behind me. On glancing back, it still hung there. Then it smiled at me—a beautiful, pleased, wholly approving smile—and faded to nothing.

I went out with Mr. Terne, and left Van alone with his father.

CHAPTER VII

One hour later I departed from the Colossus Trust Company with instructions not to return. Oh, no, I had not been ruthlessly discharged by the outraged vice president. The inhibition covered the balance of the day only, and, as Mr. Terne put it: "A few hours' quiet will give you a clearer view of the situation, Barbour. I honor you for feeling as you do. It was Richard, I believe, who obtained you a position here. Just for your consolation when Mr. Vansittart has—er—cooled off somewhat, I intend making a small plea in Richard's behalf. Now, go home and come back fresh in the morning. You look as though all the cares of the world had been dumped on your shoulders. Take an older man's advice and shake off those that aren't yours, boy!"

He was a kindly, good man, the second vice president of the Colossus. But his kindliness didn't console me. In fact, I felt rather the worse for it. I went home, wishing that he had kicked me clean around the block instead of—of liking, and petting, and by inference, praising me for being such a contrast in character to poor, reckless, loose-living, heroic Van!

When I left, the latter was still in his father's office. Though I might have waited for him outside, I didn't. He was not the kind to meet me with even a glance of reproach; but just the same I did not feel eager to meet him.

I had resolved, however, that unless Van pulled through scatheless, I would myself "make a small plea in Richard's behalf," and next time not all the smooth, smiling devils from the place-that's-no-longer-believed-in should persuade me to crumple.

On the train—I commuted, of course—I deliberately shut my eyes, and waited for the vision to appear. If it could talk to me by moving its lips, there must be some way in which I could express my opinion to it. I burned to do that. Like a sneak, it had taken me unawares in a crucial moment. I had a few thoughts of the Fifth Presence which should make even that smug vision curl up and die.

I closed my eyes—and was asleep in five minutes. I was tired, you see, and, now that I wanted it, the Fifth Presence kept discreetly invisible. The conductor, who knew me, called my station and me at the same time, and I blundered off the train, half-awake, but thoroughly miserable.

There was no one at home but my mother. Of late dad's sight had failed till it was not safe for him to be on the street alone. As he liked to walk, however, Cathy had gone out with him.

I found mother lying down in her darkened bedroom, in the preparatory stage of a headache. Having explained that Mr. Terne had given me an unexpected half-holiday, I turned to leave her, but checked on a sudden impulse.

"Mother," I said softly, "why did you name me Ser—why was I given my uncle's name instead of just dad's?"

"What an odd question"

Mother sat up so energetically that two cushions fell off the couch. I picked them up and tried to reestablish her comfortably, but she wouldn't have it. "Tell me at once why you asked that extraordinary question, Clay!"

I said there was nothing extraordinary about it that I could see. My uncle's name itself was extraordinary, or at least unusual, and the question happened to come into my mind just then. Besides, she had spoken a good deal of him lately. Maybe that had made me think of it.

Mother drew a deep breath.

"He told me—can you believe this?—he told me that some day you would ask that question! This is too wonderful! And I've seemed to feel a protecting influence about us—this house that was his—and your good position at the bank!"

"Mother, will you kindly explain what you are talking about?" My heart had begun a muffled throbbing.

"Be patient! I have a wonderful story to tell you. I've doubted, and hoped, and dared say nothing, but, Clayton, dear, in these last miserable weeks I have felt his presence like the overshadowing wings of a protecting angel. If it is true—if it only could be true—"

"Mother—please!"

"Sit down, dear. Your father never liked dear, and—why, how wonderful this all is! Your coming home early, I mean, and asking me the question just at the one time when your father, who disliked him, is away, and we have the whole house—his house!—to ourselves. Can't you feel his influence in that, dear?"

"What have you to tell me, mother?"

"I shall begin at the very first—"

"If you make the story too long," I objected craftily, "dad and Cathy will be back."

"That is true. Then I'll just tell the part he particularly wished you to know. Dear was universally loved, and I could go on by the hour about his friendships, and the faculty he had for making people happy. Physically, he had little strength, and your father was very unjust to him—"

"Can't we leave dad out of this, mother?"

"You are so like your uncle! could never bear to hear anyone criticized, no matter how the person had treated him, 'My happiness,' he would say, 'is in living at harmony with all. Clayton,' your father, he meant, of course, 'Clayton is a splendid man, whom I admire. His own fine energy and capacities make him unduly hard, perhaps, toward those less gifted. I try to console myself with the thought that life has several sides. Love—kindliness—good humor—I am at least fortunate in rousing the gentlest qualities in most of those about me. Who knows? From the beginning, that may have been my mission in life, and I was given a delicate constitution that I might have leisure merely to live, love, and be loved in return!'

"Of course, he wouldn't have expressed that beautiful thought to everyone, but knew that I would understand—yes, dear I shall come to your part in the story directly.

"—passed to his reward before you were born, my son. He went from as us in January, and you came into the world the April following. The doctors had told him that only a few hours were left him of life. When Serapion learned that he asked to be left alone with me for a little while. I remember every word of that beautiful conversation. I remember how he laid his hand on mine and pressed it feebly.

"'Do as I ask, Evelyn,' he said. 'If the child is a boy, give him my name. I only ask second place. Clayton has first right; but let the boy have my name, as well as his father's. I've been too happy in my life—too happy in my loves and friendships. I can't bear to die utterly out of this good old world. I haven't a child of my own, but if you'd just give your boy—my name. Some day he will ask why, and then you are to tell him that—it's because—I was so happy."

Mother was sobbing, but after a moment she regained self-control to continue. "You may think it weak in me to cry over my brother, who passed long ago. But he has lived in my memory. And he said: 'Some people only talk of life after death, but I believe in it. It is really true that we go out to go on. I know it. There is something bright and strong in me, Evelyn, that only grows stronger as I feel the body dying from about me. Bright, strong, and clear-sighted. I have never been quite like other men. Not even you have understood me, and perhaps that is for the best.'

"With his hand on mine he smiled, and, oh, Clayton, I have wondered many times since what that smile meant. It was so beautiful that—that it was almost terrible!

"'I love life,' he went on, 'and I shall live beyond this perishing clay. Soon or late, a day will come when you will feel my living presence in the house, and it will be in that time that your son will ask of me. Then you will tell him all I have said, and also this:

"'That I promised to return—to watch over him—to guard him.

"'Name him for me, that I may have the power. There's power in a name! And I am not as other men. Be very sure that—your son—shall be—as happy—shall have all that I've had—of life. Believe—promise!' And I promised.

"The strangest look came into his eyes. A look of—" my mother's voice sank to a hushed whisper—"I can only describe it as holy Exultation. It was too vivid and triumphant to have been of this world. And he died in my arms—Clayton, why do you look at me like that? What is the matter, child?"

"Nothing. You told the story so well that for a moment I seemed to—to see him—or Something. Never mind me. Mother, haven't you any picture of my uncle?"

"Only one of him as he was in his latter years. I have kept it locked away, for fear it might be destroyed or injured." Mother rose and started looking in a bureau drawer. "I am so glad that you take this seriously, Clayton, you feel nearly as deeply about it as I, don't you, dear?"

I wished to see that picture. At the same time I dreaded unspeakably the moment when doubt might become certainty.

My mother took out a flat package, wrapped in yellowed tissue paper. She began to undo the silk cord tied around it. I turned my back suddenly. Then I felt something thrust into my hand. With all my will I forced myself to bring the thing around before my eyes.

What face would stare back at me, eye to eye, amused, pleasant—?

The window-shades were still drawn, and the light dim. It was a moment before I realized that what I held was not a picture at all—but some kind of printed pamphlet.

"Raise the shade," said my mother. "I wish you to read that. It is a little memorial of your uncle, written by one of his friends, a Mr. Hazlett. The words are so touching! Almost as beautiful as the thoughts himself often expressed."

"Would you mind"—I controlled my voice by an effort—"would you mind letting me see the picture first?"

This time she had handed me the unmistakable, polished, bescrolled oblong of an old-fashioned photographer's mounting.

Defiance, last resource of the hard pressed, drove me in two bold strides to the window, where I jerked the shade up.

Daylight beat in. This was the middle of November and the light was gray, filtered through gray clouds. A few scattered particles of snow flickered past the window.

In my fingers the polished face of a cardboard mount felt smooth, almost soft to the touch. I watched the snow.

"Isn't his face beautiful, dear?" demanded a voice at my shoulder.

"I-I—yes, I'm afraid—of course, mother!"

"But you are not looking at it!"

"I did look," I lied. "I—this has all been a little too much for me. Take it—put it away. No, I'll read the memorial another time. Happy! Did he promise to—to come back and make me happy?"

"Practically that. How like him you are, dear son! He was sensitive, too; and your eyes! You have the Barbour nose and forehead, but your eyes—"

"Please, mother!"

She let me go at last, and in the quiet of refuge behind the locked door of my bedroom, I, who after all had not dared to look upon the picture of , scrutinized thoroughly every feature of my own face in the mirror.

Like him! She had often said so in the past, but the statement had failed to make any particular impression.

Yes, she was right about the eyes. They were the same clear, light blue as his—what? Never. Not as his. For all I knew by actual observation, 's eyes might have been sea-green or shell-pink. I had never seen him. Let me keep that fact firmly in mind.

CHAPTER VIII

My face in the mirror bore a faint sketchy resemblance to that of the unreal but none the less troublesome vision by which I was intermittently afflicted. The resemblance accounted for the vague familiarity that had enveloped it from the first.

The face in the mirror, though, was much younger, and resolve flared up in its eyes like a lighted fire.

"You," I addressed my reflection, "are not a sneak. You are not going to be made one. Tonight you will present yourself to Mr. James Barton Moore, and you will inform him that the little trick of hypnotism performed by his wife last August will either be reversed by her, or he himself will pay for it unpleasantly. I believe," and my arm muscles flexed in bravado, "that Mr. Jimmy Moore will think twice before he refuses." That was what I said. But in my heart I yearned suddenly to go and fling myself, abject, at the feet of Alicia Moore, and entreat her to help me.

It was a cold night, and the afternoon's scattered flakes had increased to a snowfall. Alighting from the car—not mine, this time, but the transit company's—I found the snow inches deep. I can still recall the feel of it blown against my face, like light, cold finger-touches.

Plowing through it, I came again to the "dead-alive house." That other visit had been in summer. The twin lawns, one green and close-cropped, the other high-grown with weeds, had stood out contrastingly then. There had been a line of sharp demarcation between Moore's clean, freshly painted half of the house and the other half's dirt-freckled wall.

Now all that sharp difference was blurred and indistinct. The snow, blue-white in the swaying circles of light from a corner arc lamp, had buried both the lawns. Joining the roofs in whiteness, drifting across the porches, swirling in the air, it obliterated all but a hint of difference between the living half and the dead.

Though the windows of one part were dark as those of the other, a faint glow shone through the curtained glazing of Moore's door.

Now that I was here, I almost hoped that he and his wife were out. The accusation I must make was strange to absurdity. I braced myself, however, opened the gate, and as I did so a hand dropped on my shoulder from behind.

A man had come upon me soundlessly through the snow. In my nerve-racked state, I whirled and struck at him.

He caught my wrist. "Here! I'm no highwayman, Clay!"

"Nils," I laughed shakily, "you startled me."

Berquist stared, with a sudden close attention that I found myself shrinking from. For weeks I had been keeping a secret at some cost. Though I had come here to reveal it, the habit of concealment was still on me.

"Your nerves used to be better than that," said Berquist shortly.

"You calling on Moore?" I queried. "Thought there was some kind of vendetta between you. You wouldn't come here with me, I remember."

"I'm glad you remember something," he retorted gravely. "You have a very nice, hospitable family, though. They took me in last night and fed me on the bare strength of my word that I'd been invited."

"I say, Nils, that's too bad."

In the desperate search I had made for Van the previous evening, I had clean forgotten my dinner invitation to Berquist. Reaching home near midnight, I had received a thoroughly sisterly call-down from Cathy, who had waited up to express her frank opinion of a brother who not only invited a friend to dinner without forewarning her, but neglected even to be present when that friend arrived.

It seemed, too, that Roberta had dined there on Cathy's own invitation, and the two girls had unitedly agreed that poor Nils was "odd" and not very desirable. He had committed the double offense of talking wild theories to dad, verbally ignoring the feminine element, and at the same time staring Bert out of countenance whenever her eyes were not actually on him.

I had informed Cathy that Bert should feel highly honored, since Nils was generally too shy even to look at a girl, much less stare at her, and that as the family's support I should certainly invite whom I pleased to dinner; as for Nils, I had regretted missing him; but knew he was too casual himself to hold the lapse against me.

Now I began an apology that was rather wandering, for my mind was otherwise concerned.

I wished to tell him about the Fifth Presence. Before I entered Moore's house, it would be very well that I should tell Nils of my errand. Why, in the name all reason, was I possessed by this sense of shame that shut my lips whenever I tried to open them concerning the haunting face?

Cutting the apologies short, Nils forgave me, explained that though out of sympathy with Moore's work, he occasionally called to play chess with him, and then we were going up the snow-blanketed walk, side by side.

Even the chess sometimes ends in "a row," Nils added gloomily. "I wouldn't play him at all, if he hadn't beaten me so many times. Perhaps some day I'll get the score even, and then I shan't come here any more."

"Moore is—did he ever tell you that I kept my appointment with him?"

"Which one?"

The question leaped out cuttingly sharp.

"The only one I ever made with him, of course. That day you introduced me to him in the restaurant."

"You haven't been coming here since?"

"No. Why should you think that?"

We had checked again, half-way up the walk. As we stood Nils caught my shoulders and swung me around till the arc-lamp rays beat on my face. He scrutinized me from under frowning brows.

"You've lost something!" he said bluntly. "I can't tell exactly what. I don't know what story your eyes hide; but they hide one. Clay, don't think me an officious meddler, but you—you have your family dependent on you—and—oh, why do I beat about the bush? That girl you will marry some day; she's rather wonderful. For her sake, if not your own, tell me the truth. Has Moore involved you in some of his cursed, dangerous experiments? Tell me, is it that, or"—his voice softened—"are you merely worn out with the common and comparatively safe kinds of trouble?"

"I've had—trouble enough to worry any fellow."

"Yes, but is any part of it to be laid at this door?" He jerked his head toward Moore's dimly radiant portal.

"A face—a face—" sheer panic choked words in my throat. I had begun betraying the secret which every atom of my being demanded should be kept.

"Yes; a face."

"A face—is not necessarily a chart of the owner's doings," I wrenched roughly from his grasp. "Since when have you set up as a critic in physiognomy, Nils?"

"When one has a friend, one cares to look beneath the surface," he said simply.

"Well, don't look with the air of hunting out a criminal, then. I have as good a right to call here as you, haven't I? Moore sent me a letter asking me to drop around, so I—I thought I would. I'm tired, and need distraction. What's the harm?"

Without answering, he eyed me through a long moment; then turned quietly and went on up into the porch.

Standing hesitant, I glanced upward, looking for a light in the windows above. Again. I saw the slanting roofs, blended in snow. Months ago, in a momentary illusion of moonlight, I had seen them look just so. The thought brought me a tiny prick of apprehension. Not fear, but the startled uneasiness one might feel at coming to a place one has never visited, and knowing it for the place one has seen in a dream.

Nevertheless, I followed Nils to the door.

Another maid opened it than the one who had admitted Roberta and myself in August. She was a great, craggy, hard-faced old colored woman, whom Nils addressed rather familiarly as "Sabina," and who made him rather glumly welcome in accents that betrayed her Southern origin. She assumed, I suppose, that Nils and I had come together, and my card did not precede me into Moore's sanctum.

The latter was in the library again. The shades and curtains were drawn tight which accounted for the "not-at-home" look of the windows from outside. I learned later that he frequently denied himself to callers, even near acquaintances, unless they came by appointment. His letter to me had been ignored too long to come under that heading. I wonder! Would he have refused to see me that night, given a choice?

In my very first step across the library's threshold, I realized that my battle was to be an even more difficult one than I had feared.

Passing the doorway I entered—physically and consciously entered—the same field of tension, to call it that, which had centralized about Alicia at the climax of my previous experience.

It was less masterful than then. There was not the same drain on my physical strength, nor the feeling of being in harmony with the movements of others. But the condition was none the less present; I knew it as surely and actually as one recognizes a marked change in atmospheric temperature or, to use a closer simile, as one feels entry into the radius of electrical force produced by a certain type of powerful generator.

There are no words which will exactly express what I mean. The consciousness involved is other than normal, and only a person who had been possessed by it could fully understand.

On that first occasion, I had been sure that my impressions were shared by the others present. This time some minutes passed before I became convinced that Berquist and James Moore, at least, were insensitive to the condition.

The library appeared as I had seen it first, save that the lamp broken then had been replaced by another, with a Japanese "art" shade made of painted silk. Near the large reading-table, with the lamp, a small stand had been drawn up and a chessboard laid on it. In anticipation of Nils' arrival Moore had been arranging the pieces. They were red and white ivory men, finely carved. They and the Japanese lampshade made a glow of exotic color, in the shadow behind which sat—Alicia, a dim figure, pallid and immobile.

By one of those surface thoughts that flash across moments of intensity, I noted that Moore was dressed in a gray suit, patterned with a faint, large check in lighter gray.

Then Moore had recognized me, and the man's pale eyebrows lifted.

"You've brought Barbour?" he said to Nils.

"No," denied my friend. "Met him at the door. How do, Alicia?"

He strode across the room to where Mrs. Moore sat in the shadow.

Under other conditions I should have felt embarrassed. By Moore's tone and Nils' non-committal response, they placed me as an intruder, received without even a gloss of welcome for courtesy's sake.

But to me it seemed only strange that they could speak at all in ordinary tones through this atmosphere of breathless tension. A voice here, I thought, should be either a shriek or a whisper.

Then Alicia's dry monotone.

"You should have come alone, Nils. You have brought one with you who is very evil. I know him. He is an eater of lives."

"Dear lady!" protested Nils, half-jokingly. "Surely you don't apply that cannibalistic description to my friend here? He might take it that way."

"How he takes it is nothing," shrugged Alicia. "There are four of us here, and there is also a fifth. And I think your friend is more aware of that than even I."

Moore's previously unenthusiastic face lighted to quick eagerness. He pounced on Alicia's original phrase like a cat jumping for a mouse.

"An eater of life! Did you say this invisible Fifth Presence is an 'eater of life,' Alicia?"

"I did not," she retorted precisely. "I said an eater of lives. Everyone does not know that—"

"No, but wait, Alicia. This is really interesting." He turned from her to us. "There's a particularly horrid old German legend about such a being." He informed us of it with the air of one imparting some delightful news. "Give me a German legend always for pure horror, but this excels the average. Der verschlingener des Lebeng—'The Devourer of Life.' Very interesting. Now the question arises, did Alicia read that yarn some time in the past, and is this the subliminal report of it coming out, or does she really sense an alien force which has entered the room in your company? What's your impression, Barbour? Have you any? You're psychic yourself—knew it the first time I saw you. Is anyone here but we four?"

By a great effort, I forced my lips to answer:

"I couldn't say. This—I—"

"Have a chair, Barbour, and take your time." He was all sudden kindliness the active sort, with a motive behind it, as I knew well enough now. To him I was not a guest but an experiment. "I haven't a doubt," he asserted cheerfully, "that you and Alicia sense a presence that entered with you and which such poor moles as Nils and myself are blind to. Now don't deny it. Anyone possessing the psychic gift who denies or tries to smother it is not only unwise but selfish. Supremely selfish. And it's a curious fact that one powerful psychic will often bring out the undeveloped potentialities in another. Alicia may have already done that for you. When you were here before—"

"That will do!" Abruptly deserting Alicia, Nils strode down upon us. There was wrath in every line of his dark face. "Jimmy, that boy is my friend! If he has 'Psychic potentialities,' as you call it, let 'em alone. He doesn't wish to develop into a ghost-ridden, hysterical, semi-human monstrosity, with one foot in this world and the other across the border."

"Really," drawled Moore, "that description runs beyond even the insolence I've learned to expect from you, Berquist. My wife is a psychic."

Nils was not too easily crushed, but this time he had brought confusion on himself. "Ghost-ridden, hysterical, semi-human monstrosity" may have been an excellent description of Alicia. It is certain, however, that Nils-had forgotten her when he voiced it. He flushed to the ears and stammered through an apology, to which Moore listened in grim silence.

Then Alicia spoke, with her customary dry directness.

"I am not offended. My guides do not like you, Nils, but that is because your opposition interferes with the work. Personally I like you for speaking frankly always. Take your unfortunate young friend, Mr. Barbour, and go away now.'

"Alicia!" Moore was half pleading, half-indignant. "You agreed with me that Barbour had possibilities of mediumship almost as great as your own. And yet you send him away. Think of the work."

"I tried to send him away the first time." From beyond the lamp Alicia's enormous eyes glinted mockingly at her husband. "You believed," she went on, "that Mr. Barbour was naturally psychic, but undeveloped. Many times, we have disagreed in similar cases. Your theory that more than half the human race might, properly trained, be sensitive to the etheric vibrations of astral and spiritual beings is true enough."

"Then why did you—"

"Don't argue, James. That tires me. I say that your belief is correct. But I have told you and, through me, my guides have told you that not everyone who is a natural sensitive is worthy of being developed."

"I consulted you"—Moore's voice trembled with suppressed irritation—"I consulted you, and you—"

"I said that a tremendous psychic possibility enveloped Mr. Barbour. That was true. Had I told you that the possibility was evil, that would have been equally true. But you would not have yielded to my judgment, and sent him away—as I tried to do."

"Alicia," cried her husband, "are we never to have any clear understandings?"

"Possibly not," she said, with cool indifference. "I am—what I am. Also I am a channel for all forces, good or evil. My guides protect me, of course. They will not let any bad spirit harm me. But I think Mr. Barbour was not glad that he stayed when I wished him to go. He has come back to me for help. I am not sure that I wish to help him. It was a long time before I was rested from my first struggle with the One he is afraid of."

Nils made an impatient movement. "I don't believe Clay needs any help except—pardon me, Alicia— except to keep away from this house and you."

"Then why did he return here?"

"Because," interpolated Moore, with a scowl for Nils, "he grew interested in his own possibilities. This attempt to frighten him is not only absurd, but the worst thing possible for him. Of course the invisible forces are of different kinds, and of course some of them are inimical. But fear is the only dangerous weapon they have. If they can't frighten you, they can't harm you."

"Alicia," cut in Nils, "seems to disagree there."

"Alicia does agree. She inclines to repel the so-called evil beings, not from fear of them, but because they are more apt to trespass than the friendlier powers. They demand too much of her strength. In consequence, I have had an insufficient opportunity to study them. If Barbour is psychic—and I should say that he very obviously is—then his strength, combined with Alicia's, should be great enough for almost any strain. You are interfering here, Berquist. I won't have it. I—will—not—have—it."

"And my friend is to be sacrificed so that you may study demonology?"

"Berquist, I have nothing to do with demons or daevas, devils or flibbertigibbets. You use the nomenclature of a past age."

"Verschlingener des Lebens," quoted Nils quickly. "You didn't boggle over nomenclature when Alicia warned us that an 'eater of life' was present."

"Oh, give me patience!" groaned Moore. "I try to trace a reference, and you—" He broke off and wheeled to the small, shadowy figure beyond the lamplight. "Alicia, exactly what did you mean when you said that an 'eater of lives' had entered the room? You can put us straight there, at least."

"I meant," drawled Alicia, "one of those quaint, harmless beings whom you are so anxious to study at anybody's expense. Not a demon, certainly, in the sense that Nils means. But not company I care for, either. No, I am not afraid of this one. He has the strength of an enormous greed—of a dead spirit who covets life—but he will not trap me again into lending my strength to his purpose.

"His! Whose? Do be plain for once, Alicia."

"I try to be," she retorted composedly. "I could give him a name that one of you at least would recognize. But that would please him too well. There is power in a name. Everyone does not know that, nor how to use it. This one does. He bears his name written across his forehead. He wills that I shall see it and speak it now. Once he surprised me into speaking it, but that was Mr. Barbour's fault. He threw me off balance at a critical moment by turning on the lights. You have probably forgotten the name I spoke then, but I doubt if Mr. Barbour has forgotten. This one whom I refuse to name has no power over me. I have many friends among the living dead who protect me from such dead spirits as this one—"

"Just a minute, Alicia!" Moore was exaggeratedly patient. "I can believe in a dead body, and through you I've come to believe in live spirits, disembodied. But a dead spirit! That would be like an extinguished flame. It would have no existence."

She shook her head. "Please don't argue, James, You know that tires me. A spirit cannot perish. But a spirit may die, and having died, exist in death eternal. There is life eternal and there is death eternal. There are the living spirits of the so-called dead. They are many, and harmless. My guides are of their number. Also there are dead spirits. They are the ones to beware of, because they covet life. Such a one is he whom I called 'an eater of lives,' and who is better known to Mr. Barbour than to me. That is not my fault, however, and now I wish no more to do with any of it. I must insist, James, that you ask Mr. Barbour to leave. In fact, if he remains in the house five minutes longer I shall go out of it."

Her strange eyes opened suddenly till a gleam of white was plainly visible all around the wide blackness of them. Her porcelain, doll-like placidity vanished in an instant.

"Make him go!" she cried. "I tell you, there is an evil in this room which is accumulating force every moment. I tell you, something bad is coming. Bad! Do you hear me? And I won't be involved in it. I won't! I won't!"

Her voice rose to a querulous shriek. A spasm twitched every feature. And then she had sunk back in her chair with drooped lids.

"Bad!" she murmured softly.

CHAPTER IX

"You will have to go, Barbour," said Moore heavily. "I am sorry, but there are occasions when Alicia must be humored. This seems to be one of them. Unfortunate. Very—unfortunate. Perhaps another time—"

He paused and glanced suggestively toward the door.

All the while that they had argued and quarreled over me, I had sat as apparently passive as the clay figure to which I had once compared Alicia. It was, however, the passivity not of inertia, but of high-keyed endurance. What Alicia felt I don't know. If it was anything like the strain I suffered under, I can't wonder that she wished to be rid of me.

"Another time," said Moore, and looked toward the door.

I rose. Instantly Berquist was beside me. He took my arm—tried to draw me away—out of the room.

I shook him off. When I moved it was toward Alicia. Before either Moore or Nils realized my objective, I was halfway around the table. Alicia, her eyes still closed, moaned softly. She cried out, and thrust forth her hands in a resisting motion:

"Stop!"

That was Moore's voice; but it was not for his sharp command that I halted. There was—it was as if a wall had risen between Alicia and me. Or as, if her out-stretched hands were against my chest, holding me back. Yet there was a space of at least two yards between us.

"What do you want, Barbour?" demanded' Moore roughly. "I said you would have to go!"

"I wish," I forced out, "to make her undo what she has done to me!"

"Then I was right!" cried Berquist indignantly.

I stood still, swept by wave upon wave of the force that willed to absorb me. The past weeks had trained me for such a struggle. Though the face of the Fifth Presence remained invisible, its identity with the intangible power I fought was clear enough to me—and I hated the face! I repulsed the enveloping consciousness of it as one strives to fling off a loathsome caress.

While I stood there, blind, silent, at war, Berquist continued:

"Now I know that I was right! Jimmy, you have let this boy suffer in some way that I neither understand nor wish wholly to understand. But believe me, you'll answer for it. Clay, lad, come away. You are courting disaster here. Alicia can't help you. She is a poor slave and tool for any force that would use her. Why, the very atmosphere of this house is contagious. Psychic. Many people are immune. Moore is immune. But I tell you, there has been more than one time when I have resolutely shut my senses against the influence, or Alicia would have dragged me into her own field of abnormal and accursed perceptiveness. It's because I resist that they won't have me at a seance. Come away!"

"No!" They could not guess, of course that I spoke from out a swimming darkness, slashed with streaks of scarlet. "No!" I muttered again. "This woman here—she can help me. She shall help me! Moore, I'll wring your neck if you don't make her help me."

Through the swimming scarlet-slashed gloom I drove forward another step. Came a rush of motion. There was a vast, muffled sound as of beating wings. A trumpet-like, voice cried out loudly: "I'll settle with you once for all!" it shouted. And then something had thrust in between Alicia and me.

Instantly the gloom lifted.

There at my right hand was the large table, with the shaded lamp and the boots and papers strewn over it. To my left the massive, empty chair in which Alicia was wont to be imprisoned during a seance.

Beyond that hung the straight, black folds of the curtains which concealed the cabinet.

Though I turned my head to neither side, I saw all these things as though looking directly at them. And also, with even more unusual distinctness, I saw what was straight ahead of me.

Between me and Alicia the figure of a man had sprung into sudden existence. In no way did this figure suggest the ghostly form one might expect from what is called "materialization." The man was real— solid.

He was of stocky, but not very powerful build. He was dressed in gray. His face—ah! Only once before had I seen this man's face with open gaze. But many times it had haunted my closed lids!

Smooth, boyish, pleasant, with smiling lips and clear, light-blue eyes—my own eyes, save that the amused gleam in them did not express a boy's unsophisticated humor.

Not a bodiless face this time, afloat in mid-air or lurking behind my lids. This was the man himself—the whole, solid, flesh-and-blood man!

I could not doubt that he was real. His hand caught my arm—roughly for all that amiable gentleness the face expressed. I felt the clutching fingers tight and heavy. He clutched and at the same time smiled, sweetly, amusedly. Clutched and smiled.

"!" I whispered. And "Serapion!"

His smile grew a trifle brighter. His clutch tightened. But I was no longer afraid of him. The very strain I had been under flung me suddenly to a height of exalted courage. Instinctive loathing climaxed in rebellion.

He clasped my left arm tight. My right was free. I had no weapon, but caught up from the table a thing that served as one.

And even as I did it, that clear side vision I have referred to beheld a singular happening. As my head grew hot with a rush of exultant blood, something came flying out through the curtains of the cabinet.

It was bright scarlet in color, and about the size of a pigeon or small hawk. I am not sure that it had the shape of a bird. The size and the peculiarly brilliant scarlet of it are all I am sure of.

This red thing flashed out of the cabinet, darted across the room, passing chest-high through the narrow space between the suddenly—embodied Fifth Presence and myself and vanished.

I heard Alicia crying: "Bad—bad! It has come!"

And then, in all the young strength of my right arm, I struck at the Fifth Presence. My aim was the face I hated. The weapon—a queer enough one, but efficient, sank deep, deep-buried half its length in one of those smiling, light-blue eyes.

He let go my arm and dashed his hand to his face. The weapon remained in the wound. From around it, even before my victim fell, blood gushed out—scarlet—scarlet. Below the edge of his clutching hand that would clutch me no more I could see his mouth, and—Heaven help me!—the lips of it smiled—still.

Then he had writhed and crumpled down in a loose gray heap at my feet.

"Barbour! For mercy's sake!"

The man I struck had sunk without a sound. That hoarse, harsh shout came from Nils. Next instant his powerful arm sent me spinning half across the room. I didn't care. He dropped to his knees. When he tried to straighten the gray heap, his hands were instantly bright with the grim color that had been the flying scarlet things.

But I didn't care!

I had killed him—it! The Fifth Presence had dared embody itself in flesh and I had slain it!

Nils had the body straight now, face upward. The light of the lamp beat down. Creeping tiptoe, I came to peer over Nils' shoulder. The lips. Did they still smile?

Then—

But there is an extremity of feeling with which words are inadequate to deal. Leave my emotions and let me state here bare facts.

The gray suit in which I had seen the Fifth Presence clothed was the same faintly checked light suit I had wondered at Moore's wearing in November.

And the face there in the lamplight, contorted, ashen, blood-smeared, was the face of James Barton Moore!

Though I had a few obscure after memories of loud talking, of blue uniforms that crowded in around me, of going downstairs and out into open air, of being pushed into a clumsy vehicle of some kind, and of interminable riding through a night cold and sharply white with snow, all the real consciousness of me hovered in a timeless, spaceless agony, whereby it could neither reason nor take right account of these impressions.

Thrust in a cell at last, I must have lain down and, from pure weariness of pain, fallen asleep. Shortly after dawn, however, I awoke to a dreary, clear-headed cognizance of facts. I knew I had killed.

When I threatened, Moore had sprung in between me and his wife, intending, no doubt with that hot temper of his, to put me violently from the house. His physical intervention had stocked me out of the shadows, then rapidly closing in, and the Fifth Presence had chosen that opportunity for its most ghastly trick.

The face I had struck at was a wraith—a vision. My weapon—one of those paper files that are made with a heavy bronze base and an upright, murderously sharp-pointed rod—had gone home in the real face behind. Instead of slaying an embodied ghost—a madman's dream—I had murdered a living man!

Last night the killing and the atrocious manner of it had been enough. This morning, thought had a wider scope. I perceived that the isolated horror of the act itself was less than all. I must now take up the heavy burden of consequences.

The hard bed on which I lay, the narrow walls and the bars that encompassed me—these were symbols by which I foreread my fate.

I, Clayton Barbour, was a murderer. In that gray, early clear-headedness I made no bones about the word or fact.

True, I had been tricked, trapped into murder; but who would believe that? Alicia—perhaps. And how would Alicia's weird testimony be received in a court of justice, even should she prove willing to give it?

I perceived that I was finished—done for. Life as I was familiar with it had already ended, and the short, ugly course that remained to be run would end soon enough.

Then for the first time I learned what the love of life is. Life—not as consciousness, nor a state of being, nor a thought; but the warm, precious thing we are born to and carry lightly till the time of its loss is upon us.

Afterward? What were dim afterwards to me? Grant that I, of all men, had reason to know that the dying body cast forth its spirit as a persistent entity. Grant that the shadow of ourselves survived the flesh. That was not life!

Let me grow old in life, till its vital flood ran low, and its blood thinned, and its flesh shriveled, and weariness came to release me from desire, Then, perhaps, I should be glad of that leap into the cold world of shadows. Now—now—I was young.

The injustice of it! I sprang up, driven to express revolt in action. For lack of a better outlet, I beat with closed fists against the wall—the bars. A lumpish, besotted creature in the cell next to mine roused and snarled like a beast at the noise.

Presently one of the keepers came tramping along the narrow alley between wall and cages.

I had retreated a little from the bars. I was not sure how this warder would look at me, a murderer. My new character was strange to me. Instinctively I shrank from being seen in it.

He peered through.

"C'm here!" he hissed softly. Puzzled, I moved nearer. "Take this!"

Then I saw that through one of the square apertures of cross-grating a folded bit of paper had been thrust. I drew it through to my side, though with no notion of what it could be. The man drew off again.

"I'll see that ya get some coffee, Barbour," he said, in a loud, offhand voice. "Morning, Mike! Early, ain't ya?" He turned to me again. "This here's Mike Megonigle. Slip him a dollar fer me as ya pass out, an' then ya won't owe me nothin'."

A red-faced, bull-necked individual had tramped into view. He stared heavily from my grating to the night warder and back again.

"Is all right, Mike," the latter asserted. "This here's Mr. Barbour. Pal of his croaked a guy last night. Barbour ain't implicated. Just a witness. He'll be getting his bond pretty quick, and when he goes out you collect that dollar for me, Mike. Can't afford to lose that dollar—not me, huh?"

He winked jovially in my direction, waved a hand on one finger of which was something which glittered brightly, and was gone. The other guard grunted, stared after him for a long minute, and moved on up the passage, still speechless and shaking his head in a slow, puzzled manner, like a bewildered ox.

But his bewilderment could not have been so great as my own. The thing that glittered on the night-guard's finger had attracted my attention before he waved it. It was a ring that had a strangely familiar look. The setting was an oval bit of lapis lazuli, cut flat, incised with a tin device the scrolls of which had been filled with gold, and surrounded by small diamonds.

Nils Berquist wore a ring like that. It was the one possession I had ever known him to prize, and that was because it had been in his family for generations. It was very old, and different from modern rings.

A duplicate? Nonsense! Why was that warder wearing Nils' ring—and what had he meant by describing me as a "witness"?

But I think some of the truth had begun to dawn on me even before I unfolded the paper that had been thrust through my grate. The inner side carried a lead-pencil scrawl, written in French. As the light in the cell was bad, and Berquist's handwriting worse, I had more than a little trouble in deciphering it.

I had read it all, however, before the return of the night-warder—that superbly corrupt official who took a bribe to deliver a message, honestly delivered it, and thereafter brazenly wore the bribe about his duties. He returned with some coffee. I was face down on the shelf that served for a bed. He rattled the grate, spoke, and as I didn't answer shoved the coffee under the door and went off—whistling, I fancy.

I couldn't have spoken to him if I had wished, because I was crying like a girl. The reaction from friendless solitude in a world made new and terrible had hit me just that way. It was not that I meant to accept Nils' sacrifice. I had not thought about the practical side of it yet. But to discover that a man who had actually seen me do that awful thing, in spite of it remained my friend and loyal to the amazing degree of taking the burden on himself—that changed the world round again, some way, and made it almost right again.

Why, the mere fact that Nils could think of me without abhorrence was enough! It restored to me all the love and friendship that had been mine and from which last night's deed had seemed to irrevocably cut me off.

If Nils, then those nearer and dearer than Nils—Roberta—But there I halted and cringed back. That way there loomed a dreadful and inevitable loss. Let contemplation of it wait awhile.

With wet eyes I sat up and again held Nils' message in the barred light that fell through the grating. He had protected his meaning by using a safer language than English—safe from the warder, at least—and couching it in terms whose real import would be obscure if it fell into other hands. At that his sacrifice was endangered in the sending, but not so much as by leaving me to blurt out the truth unwarned:

My dear Friend:

This to you, who last night were past understanding. May the morning have brought you a clear Mind. I take the chance and write. I killed James Moore. Understand me when I say this. He struck at me, but I wrested away the weapon and killed in self-defense and not in intent.

There followed a rather circumstantial account of his supposed struggle with Moore. Nils' brain had not been numbed last night, like mine. Into this story which he had made for us both to tell he had fitted the least possible fiction. Questioned on details up to almost the moment of Moore's death, we had only to stick to the truth and we could not disagree. It was a clever—a noble lie that he had arranged.

You will bear witness to all this, and they will not convict me of murder. Alicia Moore had fainted. She did not witness Moore's death. I rely on you, therefore, as my sole witness. And it is fortunate that Moore in his anger turned not on you, but attacked me! I know you, dear friend, and that you would take my place—and bear all for me, if that were possible. But I have not one in the world, save you, to suffer the anguish for my trouble. I have little to lose.

Not for your own sake, then, but for the sake of those to whom you are all—for the sake of her whose life-happiness rests with you to hold sacred or shatter, I commend you—to be glad that I and not you have this to go through with. For that I shall not think the less of you. I only ask that in your heart I beheld always as a friend.

Nils Berquist

To accept would be dishonor unthinkable.

Even the weight of the thinly veiled argument he put forward must be outbalanced by the shame of allowing an innocent man to risk the most disgraceful of deaths in my stead. I could not accept, yet though I died, the wonder of Nils Berquist's attempted loyalty should go with me—out there!

Out there! Into that dim, guessed—at coldness, with its shadowy, mocking inhabitants.

"You are right!" said a voice. "That world is to yours as the shadow to reality. But why cast the real life away?"

Had one of the warders entered my cell and addressed me, his voice could have echoed no more distinctly in my brain. Before I looked up, however, I knew what I should see. When, raising my own eyes, they met those clear, light-blue ones, I felt no surprise.

There floated the face, bodiless again, but aside from that with an appearance of substantiality which equaled—it could not exceed—that of its last tragic visitation. The undimensional flatness had given way to the solidly modeled curves of living flesh.

The point of my improvised weapon, however, had left not even a mark on the face it was meant for. That material aspect was false. Though I hated him now with an added loathing, I had learned bitterly that combat with him must be on other than physical ground. I sat sternly quiet, hoping that if I did not answer, the presence would vanish.

"Your violent temper," he continued pleasantly, but with a trace of kindly reproach, "has placed you in danger. Fortunately we—you and I—are not as other men. We need not be overborne. Tell me, which of all the forces that influence life is the strongest?"

"Hate!" Springing erect, I thrust forward till my face almost touched that of the Presence. "Such hate as I feel for you!"

He did not retreat. I could—I could almost have sworn that I felt the warmth of his flesh close to mine!

"Aw-w-w-w-, cut it out!" wailed the dweller in the next cell. "Ain't yer never goin' ter let a guy git his beauty sleep?"

"You need not speak so loud," smiled the face. "And I would suggest that you sit down. Consider the feelings of others! Consideration is a beautiful quality, and well worth cultivating. Speech between you and me need disturb no one. It can be silent as thought, for it is thought—my thought to yours. Sit down!"

A sudden weakening of the knees made me obey him. Revilings I could have withstood; curses, or threats of evil. But there was an awful sweetness and beauty in the face—a calm assurance about his preaching phrases—that frightened me as threats could not have done. Could it be that I had misjudged this serene being from beyond the border?

Then I looked in his eyes and knew that I had not. They were too like my own! I understood them. Another he might have deceived, but never me.

"Hate," he continued, in his placid, leisurely manner, "is a futile, boomerang force that invariably reacts on itself. It is the scorpion among forces, stinging itself to destruction. No; I did not come here to preach. You understand now that I spoke the truth and can read your unvoiced thoughts with perfect readiness. Our conversations are thus safe from eavesdroppers. As I was saying, hate is its own enemy and the enemy of life. There is but one invincible power, offered by God to man, and which God has commanded man to use."

"You mean—"

"Love! Armored in love, your life will be a sacred, guarded joy to you. Believe me! I am far older than I appear, and wiser than I am old. Guided by me, guarded by love, you have a beautiful future at your command."

"Begun with murder!" I snarled.

The Presence beamed patiently upon me. "That was a mistake. Don't blame yourself too severely. Blame me, if you like, though I had no idea that your foolish animosity would bring forth the red impulse of murder. Yes; we who have passed beyond can commit blunders. I made one in appearing when I did. Can't we forgive one another and forget?"

"Not while I am in jail for it and facing electrocution!" said I grimly.

"But you are not. Very shortly you will walk out a free man; under bond, it is true, but only—"

"Never!" I was on my feet again at that. "Let Nils Berquist suffer in my place? Never!"

"But he won't suffer! Or at least, not as you would. Come! Trust all that to me, who can see far, and have a certain power. Won't you trust me?"

"You mean that you can influence a jury to acquit him?"

"I have power. And think. Would you cast back his friendship in his face? Would you hurl your father into his grave, killed by horror? Would you drag your sister—your mother—through the mire of notoriety that surrounds a criminal? Would you leave them destitute? Would you stab through the very heart of the girl who loves you? Your friend has none of these to care. The opprobrium will not hurt him. He is by nature an isolated soul; and moreover, he is innocent. He has that strength, and the glory of sacrifice to sustain him. Once free yourself, you can do much to bring about his release.

"It is well known that Moore had an evil temper. The plea of self-defense will be borne out by you. Engage a clever legal advisor for your friend, and in the end your pitiful mistake will have brought harm to no one except Moore himself, who deserved it. He was a very selfish, disagreeable man! He was not loved by anyone, even his wife. What? Oh, leave Alicia out of it, my dear boy. You won't find our plans upset by her. And now, I should advise that before seekin' bondsman elsewhere, you telephone to the man whose friendship you have already won at the bank. Your immediate superior there is a kindly, good man—"

The presence got no further with his advice. As he had talked, quietly, soothingly, I had found my thoughts beginning to follow the smooth current of his. But his reference to Mr. Terne had been another of those errors to which he claimed even the disembodied were prone. It had recalled to me that scene in the president's office—Van's desperate face—and the ignominy into which I had been betrayed.

Repulsion—loathing—surged mightily through my veins again.

"No! No! No! In the name of Heaven, leave me!" I cried aloud. To my amazed relief the Presence obeyed. He had faded and gone in an instant—though by the last impression I had of him, he still smiled.

Trembling, I looked down at Nils' letter in my hand.

From the barred grating a shadow was cast upon it, and the form of that shadow was a cross.

CHAPTER X

Around 2 p.m. I was taken before Magistrate Patterson and my bail set in the sum of thirty-five hundred dollars. Arthur Terne, second vice president of the Colossus Trust Company, having appeared as my bondsman, the matter of my liberty pending the inquest, to be held the following morning, was soon arranged.

I left the court in Mr. Terne's company. Nils Berquist I had not seen, but was given to understand that he had been remanded without bail. I had pleaded in vain for a chance to talk with him.

Mr. Terne was kindness personified, though I inferred from one or two remarks that the Colossus' president was shocked.

The morning papers had featured the affair with blatant headlines. They had got my name. The Barbour & Hutchinson failure was resurrected.

The Colossus itself stalked in massive dignity across one column, irrelevantly capping a "Brutal Slaying in Haunted House," and when I saw that, I knew that "not pleased" was a mild description for Vansittart's probable emotions!

The bizarre character of Alicia, the nature of the wound, and the ghastly inappropriateness of the weapon which effected it, had appealed to the reportorial fancy with diversely picturesque results. A plain murder, with no more apparent mystery attached than this one, would have passed with slight attention. But though Alicia was not a professional medium, it appeared that she and Moore had a certain reputation.

In hinting to me of the latter's tempestuous exit from the Psychic Research Association, Nils had spared mentioning Alicia as the bone of contention. I now learned that she had been a country girl, the daughter of a hotel-keeper in a tiny Virginian village, where Moore had spent two or three autumn weeks.

Discovering in her what he regarded as supernormal powers, he wished to bring her north for further study. On her father's strangely objecting to this treatment of his daughter as a specimen, Moore had settled the difficulty by offering marriage. After the wedding, he did bring her north, educated her, and finally presented her to the Association as a prodigy well worth their attention.

Unfortunately, after several remarkable seances, she was convicted of fraud in flagrant degree. It was through the slightly heated arguments ensuing that Moore was asked to resign his directorship.

The fantastic dispute had amused the lay-public intermittently through a dull summer, but I was off in the mountains that year with Van, and what news we read was mostly on the sporting pages, whither the pros and cons of spiritualistic debate are not wont to penetrate. But all that was raked up now, as sauce for the news of Moore's sensational death, and having acquired a certain personal interest in spiritualism, I read it.

Following Mr. Terne's advice and my own inclination, I went straight home. No need to rehearse all I endured that day. Roberta's smilingly tearful consolations were the worst, I think, though, my father's: "Clay, son, you are right to stand by your friend!" ran a close second. He said it because I refused to hear a word against Nils, and insisted that the fault had not been his. Though I would not go into the details of what had taken place in Moore's library, I stuck at that one truth, and Dad, at least, who had taken a fancy to Nils the evening he dined at our house, believed me.

Altogether, however, it was a bad afternoon, and that night in my bedroom the face came again. I knew it was he, though the room was dark and I could not see him clearly. He had become so like as that to a material being!

"You have done well!" he began. "But, to make one small criticism, you must learn not to blush so easily. When your father commended your loyalty you reddened and stammered till, if you had not been among friends, suspicion might have been roused."

"My confusion only lasted a moment," I defended. Then I remembered; "You go!"

I said. "What do I want of you and your criticisms or advice? You have brought me enough unhappiness. I am a sneak and a criminal, and all through you!"

"Ingratitude is the only real crime," he retorted sententiously. "Always be grateful, and show it! You have brought unhappiness on yourself, and it is I who point the way out. So far you have followed my advice. Why turn on me now?"

"Liar!" I fairly hissed. "If you can read my thoughts, you know that I have planned otherwise than you would have me. I am doing as Nils wished without regard to you, and not for the sake of myself. And let me tell you this! If there arises the slightest prospect that my friend will not be cleared, I shall confess. Tomorrow will decide it. If things go badly for him at the inquest, my people will have to suffer. The shame and loss he is trying to save them from would be nothing, then, to the shame involved by silence!"

Had the face possessed shoulders, I know he would have shrugged them.

"You are wrong, but we need not discuss that. I tell you in advance that your friend will be held for willful murder. Did you know quite all that I know, you would not hope for a different indictment."

The strings of my heart contracted. I passed a breathless moment of realization. Then: "Tomorrow I confess!" I said firmly.

"Tomorrow you will choose a lawyer for your friend, and begin the work which will surely achieve his release."

"You do not know that. You have admitted that you are capable of mistakes."

"Not in a case of this kind. I possess a wide knowledge of facts which enables me to be very sure that your friend will get his release. I am your unswerving ally. And remember that I have not only wisdom, but some power.

"Oh, you are—leave me!" I cried aloud. "In God's name go!"

The faintly, seen oval of his smooth face faded, though more slowly than in the cell at the station-house.

I heard a soft swish of slippered feet in the hall. Someone rapped lightly and opened my door.

"Clay, dear," said my mother, "did you call? Are you ill?"

"No. I had a bad dream and awoke crying out because of it."

"One can't wonder at that." She came and sat on the edge of my bed. "Such an awful thing for you to be in! Please, dear son, keep to your own class after this. Trouble always comes of mingling with queer Bohemian people who have no standards, or—or morals."

"Nils Berquist has the highest standard of any—man I know!" I was fiercely defensive.

There was a pause of silence. Then in the dark she leaned and kissed my forehead. "You are so like him!" she murmured.

I groaned. "If only that were true!"

"But you are. With those blue, clear eyes of his, that saw only beauty and love. He would never hear a word against a friend."

"Mother! You meant that I am like—"

"'Your uncle, yes. And in some strange way I feel sure that his guarding influence is really about us. Why, when I came into the room just now I had the queerest feeling—as if it were a room in a dream, or—no, I can't convey the feeling in words. But the sense of his presence was in it. I do truly believe that he has returned to guard us in the midst of so much trouble. At least, it would be like him. Dear, faithful, loving, lovable!"

But had my desired obsession, or familiar, or haunting ghost really desired to help, he might have warned me definitely of Sabina Cassel.

Alicia did not appear at the inquest. She was ill and under a physician's care. Her semi-conscious state as reported by him prevented even the taking of a deposition.

I did not, however, stand alone as star witness before the coroner's jury. Sabina Cassel, Mrs. Moore's old colored "Mammy" whom she had brought north with her from Virginia, shared and rather more than shared the honors with me.

They had taken pains that Nils and I should not meet. He was kept rigorously incommunicado till the inquest, no one, save the police and the district attorney, having access to him. At the inquest I caught only a glimpse of him, when he was led out past where I awaited my turn before the jury. Involuntarily I sprang up, only to be caught by a constable's hand, while Nils was hustled out. As he went, he threw me a glance that was a burning, dictatorial command.

I obeyed it. I told the jury exactly that story which Nils' letter had outlined for us both. There was tempered steel in Berquist.

I could be sure that no long-drawn torment of inquisition could make him vary a hairsbreadth from the line he had set for us to follow.

In my testimony, which preceded Sabina's, I explained that Nils had objected to my interest in spiritualism, fostered by a single previous visit to the Moores' place. That he wished me to leave the house with him, and that Alicia also had seemed set against my remaining. That an argument ensued, at the height of which Moore became very angry and excited, shouted: "I'll settle with you, once for all!" and came around the table toward Berquist.

"He grasped Berquist's arm," I said.

"When my friend tried to free himself, Moore snatched the—the file from the table. I saw Berquist seize Moore's wrist. They struggled a moment, and then Moore staggered away—with his hands to his face. Then—he fell down. Berquist called to me, and, no, I had not tried to interfere. It all happened too quickly. There wasn't time. After Berquist wrenched the file from Moore's hand I don't believe he struck at Moore. I think the file was driven into his eye by an accident."

That surmise, of course, was struck from the record; but I had said it, at least, and hoped it impressed the jury.

"Afterward, the—the sight of blood and the suddenness of it all turned me sick—no, my recollections were clear up to that time."

And so forth. It was a straight story. I knew it agreed to a hair with Nils' confession.

What I did not, could not know, was that it varied in one essential detail from an entirely different confession—a confession made by a person whom we had not considered as an even possible eye-witness, and whose very existence I, at least, had forgotten.

Given that a second eyewitness existed, one would have supposed that the disagreement would have been over the slayer's identity. It was not. By a curious trick of fate, Sabina Cassel, Alicia's old colored maid, did undoubtedly see me strike Moore down, and yet, not through such a super-normal illusion as caused me to kill Moore, but in a perfectly natural manner, she had confused Berquist's identity with mine. She related as having been done by Berquist that which had been done by me.

In one detail only did Sabina's testimony conflict with ours, but that was the kind of detail which would hang a man, if its truth were established.

She had seen me—Berquist by her own account—snatch the file from the table and strike Moore, and she had seen me do it on no further provocation than the laying of Moore's hand on my arm.

The Fifth Presence was right when he foretold that Nils would be indicted.

And yet, though things had indeed gone ill for Nils at the inquest, I did not at once carry out my expressed intention and substitute myself for him as defendant.

I didn't wish to die, nor spend years in prison. I wanted to live and have a decent, straight, pleasant future ahead, such as I had been brought up to expect as a right. It seemed to me that just one way lay open. Though Nils was now entirely at my mercy, only his untrammeled acquittal would give me the moral freedom to keep silent. For that a first-class lawyer was an absolute necessity.

Berquist was practically penniless, and the Barbour exchequer in not much better state. Here again, however, friendship came to the fore in a curiously impressive manner. For the sake of an old acquaintance and some ancient friendly claim that my father had on him, none other than Helidore Mark, of Mark, Mark & Orlow, who could have termed himself Mark the famous and not lied.

I remember my fast interview with him after dad had—to me almost incredibly—persuaded him into alliance. My first impression was of a mild-looking, smallish man, with a scrubby mustache. He had hurt the top of his bald head in some way, so that it was crossed with a fair-sized hillock of adhesive plaster. I thought that added to insignificant appearance; but he had the brightest, softly brown eyes I have ever seen, and after the first few minutes I was afraid of him.

I was afraid that I would tell him too much.

My confidence, however, proved not the easily uprooted kind of a common criminal, and for Nils the acquisition of this famous, insignificant looking lawyer gave me the only real hope of assurance I had through those bad days.

"Your friend," Mark had said to me, "is a rather wonderful young man; Barbour. I can't blame you for being troubled. He has the kind of intelligence that would make a legal genius of him, if he had turned his efforts in that direction. A wonderful intelligence—and all lost in a maze of impractical theorizing and the sort of dreams that can't come true so long as men are men, and women are women, Heaven help us all! He shan't go to the chair, nor prison, either. He's my man, my case, and—yes, I'll say my friend, though I don't run to sudden enthusiasm. Leave Berquist to me!"

Evidently, Mark's consultations with his case had not been kept within strictly professional bounds. I smiled involuntarily. I could picture that long dark face of Nils lighting to alert interest as he discovered that Mark was not merely the lawyer who might save him from martyrdom, but also a thinking man. He must have brought out a side of the little man that was kept carefully submerged at ordinary times. I am sure that few people had seen Helidore Mark inclined to dilatory wanderings in philosophy, such as Nils loved.

But I went out with a lighter heart and more optimism than I had carried in some time. Mark, with his "my man, my case, my friend!" had installed a confidence which remained with me all that day.

I had returned to the bank, for though I walked in the Valley of the Shadow, while I could walk I must work.

So Mr. Terne had me back again, and it was a very good thing that I had Mr. Terne to go back to. Not many men would have put up with the abstracted attention my work received, nor patiently picked up the slack of details I let go by me.

His patience had a characteristic reason behind it, which I was sure of from the minute he told me about poor Van.

The latter, it seemed, had really gone the step too far with his father in the affair of Mr. Terne's four hundred. Vansittart, Sr., would let no one speak of his son to him after that day. Everyone in the bank, however, knew that he had quarreled with him, disowned him, and that Van, in a fit of temper, had refused the offer of a last money settlement—a couple of thousand only, it was said—flung out of the Colossus, and walked off, leaving the gray roadster forlorn by the curb.

No one knew where Van had gone after that. He had simply vanished, saying no goodbyes, and taking nothing with him but the clothes he wore.

Mr. Terne felt guilty because it was his complaint which had caused the final rupture. He liked me, anyway, but having, as he believed, ruined Van, he showed an added consideration for me which developed into an almost absurd tenderness for my feelings.

He needed that, if I was to be kept on the tracks at all those days. I was nervous as a cat, and ready to jump at the creak of a door.

Roberta would watch me with wide, troubled eyes, and because a question was in them I would grow irritable and fling off and leave her with almost brutal abruptness. And always she forgave me—till I came near wishing she would forgive less easily.

Cathy resented my new irritability with the merciless justice of a sister; mother endured my anxiety for Nils only because it proved I was like "dear," and dad harped on his pride in me for "standing by" till I really dreaded to go near him.

As for the Fifth Presence, he remained detestably faithful. Several times I explained to him that if Nils were not cleared I intended to confess. When he only continued to smile, I ceased talking to him.

He still came, however, and on the very night before the trial opened, the last thing of which I was conscious, dropping asleep, was his smooth, persuasive, hateful, silent voice. As ever, it was expressing the platitudinous—and always subtly evil—advice to which habit had so accustomed me that it had grown very hard indeed to distinguish his speech from my thoughts!

CHAPTER XI

When a murderer—for I named myself—is called to confront across some feet of court-room the innocent man standing trial in his stead, he needs all his nerve and a bit more to keep steady under the questioning of even a friendly and considerate counsel.

In fact, I was strangely more afraid of Mark than of District Attorney Clemens. I might, however, have spared myself there.

The impaneling of the Jury had been a battle-royal between Mark and Clemens, at which I was not present, but which had roused the newspaper men to gloating anticipation (the real battle to follow).

Then Mark became ill—dropped out!

I could hardly believe it when Orlow, his junior associate, met me on the first day of the trial, and broke the news. A brain tumor caused by the injury.

Had it not been for Mark, I told myself, I would never have let Nils Berquist go to trial. Should I allow it to go on now, with our best hope hors de combat?

The second Mark, Helidore's brother, was in Europe, and Orlow, while brilliant in his fashion, was not a man to impress juries. His genius lay in the hunting out of technical refinements of law, 'ammunition,' as it were, for the batteries which had brought rage to the heart of more than one district attorney.

When he arose presently in court and asked for a delay in proceedings, Clemens' eye lighted. When Mr. Justice Ballington refused the request—a foregone conclusion, because Mark, admittedly, was in too serious a condition for the delay even to be measured—Clemens lowered his head suddenly. It might have been grief for his adversaries' misfortune—or, again, it might not.

Where I sat with other witnesses, I was intensely conscious of an absurd, brilliantly veiled little figure, two chairs behind me.

This was my first glimpse of Alicia, since the night of Berquist's arrest. Though I knew Mark had been granted at least two interviews with her, me she had resolutely refused to receive.

Now I was relieved to find that her nearness brought no return of the supernormal influence I had suffered before in her vicinity.

She sat stiffly upright, and did not glance once in my direction. Perhaps her 'guides' had advised her to don that awful veil of protecting purple for this occasion, or she may have worn it as a tribute to her husband's memory. It certainly gave her a more unusual appearance than would a crape blackness behind which a newly made widow is wont to hide her grief.

At her side towered the large form of Sabina Cassel.

The trial opened.

One Dr. Frick appeared on the stand, and in elaborate incomprehensibility described in surgical terms the wound which had caused Moore's death. I saw him handling a small, hideous object—gesturing with it to show exactly how it had been misused to a deadly purpose.

Then for several minutes I didn't see anything more. Luckily all eyes in the courtroom were on either the doctor or the "murderer." Nobody was watching me.

The doctor's demonstration seemed to prove rather conclusively that my "accident" hypothesis was impossible. The file, he showed, could have been driven into the brain only by a direct blow.

Dr. Frick was allowed to stand down.

In establishing the offense, Clemens saw fit to call Alicia herself.

As her mistress arose, Sabina's massive bulk stirred uneasily, as if she would have followed her to the stand.

At the inquest, the old colored woman's testimony had done more than cause Nils' indictment for murder. It had made a public and very popular jest of Alicia's claim to intercourse with "spirits." But though, in the first flush of excitement over Moore's death, Sabina had betrayed her, the woman was loyal to her mistress. When a murmur that was almost a titter swept the packed audience outside the rail. Sabina shook her head angrily, muttering to herself.

The audience hoped much of Alicia, and its keen humor was not entirely disappointed. No sooner had she appeared than an argument began about her preposterously brilliant veil. The court insisted that it should be raised. Alicia firmly declined to oblige. She had to give in finally, of course, and when that peaked, white face with its strange eyes was exposed, the hydra beyond the rail doubtless felt further rewarded.

The hydra believed her a fraud. They had reason. I, with greater reason, understood and pitied her!

I thought she might break down on the stand. Alicia's character, however, was a complicated affair that set her outside the common run of behavior. To Clemens' questions she replied with sphinx-like impassivity and the precision of a machine.

Her answers only confirmed Nils' story and mine to a certain point, and stopped there. There was not a word of "sprits" nor "guides;" not a hint of any influence more evil than common human passions; not a suggestion, even that she had formed an opinion as to which man, slayer or slain, was the first aggressor. I am sure that a more reserved and non-committal widow than Alicia never took the stand at the trial of her husband's supposed murderer.

"James," she said, "wished Mr. Barbour to remain. Mr. Berquist wished him to leave. They argued. No, I should not have called the argument a quarrel—I did not see Mr. Berquist strike James. While they were talking I lost consciousness of material surroundings. Yes, my loss of consciousness could be called a faint. The argument was not violent enough to frighten me into fainting. Yes, there was a reason for my losing consciousness. I lost consciousness because I felt faint, I was tired. I do that sometimes. Yes, I warned them that something bad was coming. I couldn't say why. I just had that impression. I did not see either James or Mr. Berquist assume a threatening attitude—"

Released at last, she readjusted her purple screen with cold self-possession, and returned to her seat.

It was Sabina Cassel's next turn. Save in appearance, Alicia had not after all come up to public anticipations. In Sabina, however, the hydra was sure of a real treat in store.

Judge Ballington rapped for order. Sabina took her oath with a scowl. Every line of her face expressed resentment.

But she was intelligent. To Clemens' questions, she gave grim, bald replies that offered as little grip as possible to public imagination.

Yes, on the evening in question she had been standing concealed behind the black curtains of "Miss 'Licia's" cabinet, or "box," as Sabina called it. No, "Marse James" did not know she was there. Miss 'Licia and she had "fixed it up" so that one could enter the box from the back. Marse James had the box built with a solid wooden back, like a wardrobe. It stayed that way—for a while.

"Then Marse James he done got onsatisfied. Yas, de sperits did wuhk in de box an' come out ob it, too; but Marse James, he ain't suited yit. He want dem 'sperits shud wuhk all de time! He neber gib mab poh chile no res'!"

And so Alicia, who, according to Sabina, could sometimes but not always command her "sperits," devised a means to satiate Moore's scientific craving for results.

While he was absent in another city, the two conspirators brought in a carpenter. They had the cabinet removed and a doorway cut through the plastered wall into a large closet in the next room. By taking off the cabinet's solid back and hanging it on again, it would just open neatly into the aperture cut to fit it. Alicia kept plenty of gowns hung over the opening in the closet beyond.

Returning, Moore found his solid-backed cabinet apparently as before. From that time, however, the "sperits" were more willing to oblige than formerly.

"Ab uno disce omnes," is invariably applied to the medium or clairvoyant caught in fraud, though translated: "From all fraud, infer all deceit."

The world laughed over the "spiritualistic fake again exposed!" I did not laugh.

Let it be that the hand which Roberta and I had seen was Sabina's gnarled black paw, and that my impression of its unsubstantiality was a self-delusion. Let those strange little twirling flames that had arisen pass as the peculiar "fireworks" I had tried to believe them. Let even the incident of the broken lamp have been a feat of Sabina's—though how her large, clumsy figure could have stolen out past the table and into the room unheard was a puzzle—and the masculine voice wonderful ventriloquism.

Grant all these as deceptions. There had come that to me through Alicia's unwilling agency which had given me a terrible faith in her, that no proof of occasional fraud could dispel.

Clemens' interrogations touched lightly on the object of the door in the cabinet's supposedly solid back, only serving to establish the fact that it was possible for his witness to have been practically in the library unknown to all the room's other occupants save, probably, Alicia.

Then he asked Sabina's story of that night in her own words. She began it grimly:

"Waal, Ah wuz in behin' de cuhtins dat hangs in front ob Miss 'Licia's box. Dem cuhtins is moderate thin. Ah cudn' see all dey is in de room, but Ah suttinly cud see all dat pass in front ob de lamp. Yass, dat whut yoh got in yoh hand am one a dem cuhtins."

Here Clemens checked her, while the "cuhtin," was passed from hand to through the jury-box. Each juryman momentarily draped himself in mourning while he assured himself that it was thin enough to be seen through. Then with solemn nods Exhibit B was restored to the district attorney. Sabina continued.

"Dese yeah germnen, Mistah Buhquis' and Mistah Bahbour, dey come in, and right away de argifyin' stahted. Ah kain't tell all dey, say. Dey use high-falut in', eddicated laniguige what am not familiar toh me, tho' Lawd knows Ah's done hear enuff ob it 'sence Miss 'Licia come norff wif Marse James Mooah."

"Dey argifies an' argifies. Mistah Bahbour, he don't say nuffin' much. But Mistah Buhquis', he specify dey shud bof up'n leave. Miss 'Licia she say mebbe sump'n bad gwine happen purty quick. Marse James, he say: 'Mistah Bahbour, you go; come back 'notha time.' Mistah Bahbour, he say no, he doan wanta go, kaze Miss 'Licia c'n mebbe help him some way. Mistah Buhqus' he go right up in de aih. He specify some hahm done come ob he fren' stayin roun' deah any longah.

"Mistah Buhquis' he am standin' right alongside de big table wif de lamp on it. De lamp am behin' him. I see ebery move he make.

"He done muttah sump'n low. Ah don't rightly know what he say, but it hab a right spiteful, argifyin tone to it.

"'Marse James,' he holler out: 'I fix yoh now foh dat!' an' he rush obah to Mistah Buhquis' an' lay han' on he arm—No, suh; he didn't go foh to do Mistah Buhquis' no hahm. Marse James he hab a way ob talkin' loud an' biggety, but Ah nevab done saw him do no hahm to nobuddy.

"He grab Mistah Buhquis' lef' arm. Mistah Buhquis', he reach out he otha' han' and grab sumpn off de table. Marse James don' do nuthn'. Mistah Buhquis,' he fro back he han' an' hit out wif it real smaht. Marse James leggo de ahm, clap he han's obah he face, an' sorta lets go all obah. He jes' crumble down lak.

"Ah knows dat de bad am happen.

"Ah cuddin' git out dat box easy into de room, kaze dey's a table in it dat reach purty nigh acrost, an' Ah ain't spry to climb ober it. No, suh; Ah didn't thin to shov de table out de way. Ab cain't think ob nuffin' but Miss 'Licia. Ah turns roun' an' gits out de back, kaze Ah wants to git to an mah Miss 'Licia. Ah comes roun' to de hall and goes in de library. Deah is Mistah Buhquis' stannin' obah Marse James, he han's all drippin' blood.

"Ah say: 'Yo' done kill him, ain't yoh?'

"He luks all roun' kinda pitiful lak, an' then he say:

"'Yas, Sabina, Ah kill him! Now go fotch de doctah an' some p'leece!'

"Mistah Buhquis', he am lak lots ob otha high-spirited gernmen. He don't go foh to kill Marse James, but when Marse James tech him in anger, he jes' bleeged foh to do it—Das all right! Ah gotta right to hab mah 'pinion, same as ebryone. Waal, don't put it in de writin' record, den. Ah don' keer whut yoh does. Das jes' mah 'pinion!

"Yas suh. Ah's suah dat it war Mistah Buhquis' grab de file and not Marse James. Wall, Marse James, he stann wif he lef' side to de table. Yas, suh; I cud suah nuff tell which wuz which. Marse James, he ain't so tall by purty nigh a fut high as Mistah Buhquis'. It am de tall man who start' wif de right side ag'in' de table who take de file off'n it. No; Marse James don' try ter do nuffin hurtful to Mistah Buhquis'. No; dey don' struggle roun' none atall. Dey jes' stan' deah. Its de Lawd's truf, dat was de mos' onexcitin' killin' Ah hab evah saw!"

And then Clemens let her go, to the deep disgust of Hydra, outside the rail. He had not asked what she was doing in the cabinet, nor many other of the questions which gave an amusing double interest to the Moore murder. All that, however, was bound to come out in the cross-examination, and, meantime, Sabina had proved "Clemens' witness" to an extent which made the case promise well of interest on its tragic side.

I was not called before the jury until after the noon recess, which gave me time to think things over a bit more.

At the inquest, I had not actually heard Sabina's testimony. Though Mark, who interviewed her as well as her mistress, had warned me that she would prove a difficult antagonist, I had not fully believed him. She had seemed ill-educated, the type whose average run are diffuse in their statements and easily muddled into self-contradiction.

Sabina might prove so under cross-examination, but I doubted it now. She had wasted hardly a word that morning, and there was only one point on which I was sure that she could be shaken.

The difference in height between slayer and slain was a strong point for the prosecution. Even through thin, black curtains it would indeed have been hard to confuse a tall silhouette with a short one. But no one had thought to question the identity of the tall silhouette.

Though Sabina may have known better during the minutes that she stood staring through the curtains, her after and more vivid sight of Berquist, hands "dropping blood," and his almost instant claim of the crime as his own, had served to make the tall man Berquist in all her memories.

Berquist, the self-confessed!

I had no faith in Orlow. Had Mark not dropped out, I should have been content to let the trial take its course, sure that his genius would somehow save the day and free my friend. But under Orlow's handling, with that craggy, sullen, assured black woman to swear that Moore was not and could not have been the aggressor—since he stood with his left side to the table, grasping the tall silhouette with his right hand, and a man under impulse of passion is not likely to reach for a weapon with his left—I was morally certain that Berquist would lose out.

But what if, rising on the stand, instead of a second perjury I told the simple truth?

Not that portion of it which included the superhuman, but just the fact that I, and not Berquist, had been swept by one of those sudden fits of red anger that have made murderers of many before me?

Why, Sabina herself would support my words, once spoken! There was a little, unnoticed twist in her testimony—a point where the voice of Berquist, coming from beyond the table, became the voice of the tall man standing on her side of the lamp.

The instant that I spoke she would know. Her memories, unconsciously readjusted to fit facts as she had afterward learned them, would be straight again. Berquist's hidden heroism would stand revealed, and I, though I died, I would at least die clean.

Resolve crystallized suddenly within me. When Clemens called me to the stand I would go, not to testify, but to confess.

I walked to the little raised platform, with the chair where the others had sat, below the double tier of jurymen. I mounted it. Somebody put a dusty black book under my hand and mumbled through a slurred rigmarole, to which my low acquiescence was a prelude to ruin for me. I sat down in the chair.

Beyond the rail was a packed level of faces. They were all pale and dreary looking, it seemed to me, though that may have been an effect of light, for the day was gray and dreary. I had returned to court through falling snow. It was a wet, late spring fall of clinging flakes, and all the way I had been haunted by a memory of the "dead-alive" house as I had seen it that night.

Not the interior—not even the library, with its master, a grim gray and scarlet horror on the floor. But the house itself, desolate under its white burden, with the great flakes swirling down, hiding deeper and more deep the line of division between the living hall and the dead.

Berquist was sitting by a table with Orlow beside him. I had visited him in prison, of course, and talked with him a few moments just before the trial opened. His determination and courage had never swerved, nor his conviction that we had only to keep steady and win.

Now I saw his eyes as a dark and valiant glory fixed on me. Their message only hardened my resolve. That man to play the martyr for my sake? Never!

Orlow left Nils, and took his stand conveniently near. He was there to protect me from irrelevant questions, but he looked quite out of place. Clearly, the mantle of Helidore Mark did not rest easily on his shoulders.

The district attorney, a thin, scholarly person whom I instinctively disliked, began his inquisition.

"Your name, please? Age and occupation?"

"Barbour—Clayton S. Barbour," I corrected myself. "I am—"

"Just a moment. Your full name for the record, please, Mr. Barbour."

Clemens, who would reserve any attempt to "rattle" me for my appearance in the rebuttal, was politeness itself.

"Clayton— Barbour!" I forced out. Then I cursed myself for not having substituted "Samuel," or left out the initial.

"There's power in a name." Once I would have laughed at that statement, but not now. Not with my recent memories.

And as God is my witness, I sat there and saw the district attorney's hatchet-face change, blend, grow smooth and loathsomely pleasant.

Clemens continued his interrogations, but I spoke to another than he when I answered them.

The living bound by the dead!

CHAPTER XII

May 15

Mr. C. S. Barbour.

Sir: I am writing to you because my guides advise it. Otherwise I should not do so. I have returned to my old home in Virginia. The newspapers were very cruel to me, as you know, and everyone unkind and harsh and disbelieving.

James understood me. If he had found out about the cabinet, he would have been annoyed, but he would only have taken more pains after that to see that all the phenomena were genuine. I can't help doing such things. It is a part of my nature. James said I was very complex.

In a measure, it is your fault that he left me. I am not vengeful, however, and I do not hold it against you, because I can very well guess at what you had to contend with. For some cause that has not yet been revealed to me—some cause within yourself, I fear—you were and still are peculiarly open to the attack of one we know of.

Were yours an ordinary case of obsession, I might have helped. As it is, I can only offer warning. Whatever there is in you that answers to him, choke it—crush it back—give it no headway. Above all, do not obey him. If, as I suspect, you have obeyed in the past, cease now. It is not yet too late. But if June 9 finds you under his domination you will never be free again.

You may wonder why I was silent at the trial. You may have thought that I was ignorant of the truth. This is not so, though I did not even tell Sabina. To bring the greater criminal to justice was impossible. For the rest, it was between you and your friend.

Understand, I will not interfere between you and your friend.

My guides say that this is not for me to do. That I must not. That if one of you wills to sacrifice and the other to accept; not even God will interfere between you.

But I write particularly to give this message.

Mortal life is cheap, and mortal death an illusion. Beyond and deeper are Life and Death eternal. Be careful which you choose.

Alicia Moore

CHAPTER XIII

"Plain life and death are the only realities. Life eternal—death eternal! For you and me, those are words, my boy—just words!"

It was dusk in my room. I sat on the edge of the bed, chin in hands, staring at the inevitable companion of my solitude. At my feet lay the scattered sheets of Alicia's letter, scrawled over in a large, childish hand. The outside world was bright with an afterglow of the departed sun. But gray dusk was in my room.

"Just words," repeated the face.

"Just words," I said after him dully. Then, at a thought, I roused a trifle. "He won't go through with it. Even Nils Berquist can't be willing to die without a protest—and for such a crawling puppy as would let him do it."

"He will die, but not entirely for your sake," the presence retorted.

"What do you mean?"

"You haven't guessed? Well, it is rather amusing from one viewpoint. Your friend is not only in jail; he's in love!"

"Nils? Nonsense! Besides, if he were in love he would wish to live, not die!"

"That is the amusing part. He is willing to die, because of the love."

"Some woman refused him, you mean?"

"No; the girl is not even aware of his feeling toward her. She would, I think, be shocked at the very thought. He has only spoken with her twice in his life. But from the first moment that he saw her face he has loved her. He has sat in the courtroom and watched her while the lawyers fought over his life, and to his peculiar nature—rather an amusingly peculiar nature, from our viewpoint—merely watching her so has seemed a privilege beyond price. He is willing to die, not for you, but to buy her happiness."

"Who is this girl?" I asked hoarsely, and speaking aloud as I still sometimes did with him.

"You should know."

"Nils Berquist—in love—with Roberta?" I said slowly. "But that's absurd. You are lying!"

"No. Every day, as you know, she was in that audience beyond the rail. For your sake. Because she knew how you cared for this man Berquist. She herself has a shrinking horror of the 'red-handed murderer,' but her devotion to you has served our purpose well. That first mere glimpse he had of her on the street—the hour at dinner in your house—these impressions might have somewhat paled in the stress of confronting so disgraceful a form of death. But in the courtroom he watched her face for hours every day, and each day bound our dear poet and dreamer tighter."

"But—"

"He measures her love for you by his own for her. As you are his friend still, uncondemned and worthy, he will buy your life for her."

"He loves her—and would have her marry a murderer?"

"He believes as you have told him, and truly enough, that you were thrown off balance by some influence connected with Alicia and did not know what you, were doing. But it is rather amusing, as I said. He loves the girl for the goodness and purity of her beauty, and for her newly born sadness. You have tired of her for the same reasons, and plan to break the engagement. But he needn't know that, eh?"

"Liar! I shall marry Roberta."

"When? Never! No; you are entirely right. She is not the wife for you. With my help you can easily attract a better. I know at least one woman among your mother's friends who is already devoted to you, and who has means to make not only you but your whole family happy and comfortable. I mean the blond widow, who owns the big house next to your old home. What is her name? Marcia Baird. Yes; she is the woman I refer to. Oh, I knew she's over thirty, but think what she could give you. As for the girl, she knows your circumstances. Her love is selfish, or she would have released you before this."

"You are lying, as you have lied in the past."

"What have I said that proved untrue?"

"You have lied from the first. There was poor old Van. You said that his father would forgive him, and he didn't."

"Be fair. You misquote. I said that Van would not be ruined. With the enthusiastic despair of youth, he played hobo for a while. Then he went to work at the one thing be understood. He is a very industrious mechanic now in an automobile factory with good chances of a foremanship, and—except for grease— living cleaner than he ever did before. He was going the straight down road, but his sacrifice for you pulled him up. You will hear from him shortly. He doesn't bear you any grudge."

"You promised to be my ally; to use your power as an influence to help."

"I kept the promise. Has the least slur of suspicion fallen upon you? Is not every one your friend? Is there a man or woman living who hates or despises you? Are you not shielded and sheltered by the mantle of love, as I foretold?"

"But you promised that Nils would be acquitted."

"Not acquitted. I said released. For such a spirit as his, this world is a prison. In real life, such as you and I prize, there is no contentment for him. Death will release him to that higher sphere where the idealist finds perfection, and the dreamer his dreams. Believe me, Nils Berquist could never be happy on earth. In speeding his departure, we are really his benefactors—you and I."

The face beamed as though in serene joy for the good we had done together; but I hid my head in my arms, groaning for the shame of us both.

June 9 was coming. June 9.

CHAPTER XIV

June 5

My Dear Clayton:

Mother has told me of your talk with her. I am glad to learn that your views coincide with my own, as I have felt for some time that it would be best for me to release you from our engagement. Your ring and some gifts I return by the messenger who carries this. I am leaving shortly on a visit to friends of mother's in the South, so we shall not meet again soon. Wishing you the best of fortune in all ways, I remain.

Very truly yours.

Roberta Ellsworth Whitingfield.

June 5

My Own Dearest—Here and Hereafter:

Mother didn't understand as I do. She made me write the letter that goes with this. She is very proud, and that you should be the one who wished to break our engagement shamed her. She even believed a gossip that you have been paying court to Mrs. Marcia Baird on the sly. I had to laugh a little. Imagine it! If I could picture you as disloyal, I could never, I'm sure, picture you making love to that poor, dear, sentimental, rich Mrs. Baird, who is old enough to be the mother of us both. Well, maybe not quite that, but awfully old. Thirty-five, anyway.

But mother half believed it, and to please her I wrote that cold, hard letter that goes with this.

I'm not proud a bit, dearest. I have to tell you that I understand. You are burdened to the breaking-point; but it is I whom you wish to free, not yourself. Dearest, I don't want that kind of freedom. Love is sacrifice. Don't you know that I could wait for you a lifetime, if needs be? Mother says you never truly loved me, or you would not let me go. I know better. We are each other's only, you and I. I measure your love for me by mine for you, and, if it's years or a lifetime, be sure that I shall wait.

You have suffered so over this terrible tragedy of your friend that I can't bear you to have even a little pain from doubt of me. It seems dreadful that I should leave you on the very day before—before June 9. But mother has bought the tickets and made all the arrangements, so I must go. I won't hurt you by saying a word against your friend; but oh, my dearest, don't quite break that heart I love over a tragedy that, after all, isn't yours. You have been to him all that a friend could be. True—loyal—self-sacrificing.

You could not have done or suffered more if he had been your brother. That's one reason I am sure of you, dearest. No man who could be so loyal to friendship will ever forget his love.

I promised mother not to see you again, but nothing was said about letters! I'll send you an address later. Clay, darling, goodbye till you are free to take me.

Remember—years or a lifetime

Your own dearest always, here and hereafter

Bert

June 8

(Extract from Evening Bulletin)

...Truck collides with taxi on Thirty-Second Street. Miss Roberta Whitingfield victim of fatal accident.... Early this morning a heavy truck, loaded with baggage, skidded across a bit of wet asphalt on Thirty-Second Street, and collided with the rear of a taxicab traveling in the same direction. The taxi was hurled against the curb.... One of the occupants uninjured ... daughter, Miss Roberta Whitingfield taken to St. Clement's Hospital ... death ensued shortly afterward.... Miss Whitingfield said to have been the fiancee of Clayton S. Barbour, a witness in the famous Moore murder trial, and who has since vainly exerted himself to obtain a pardon for the murderer, Berquist.... If the victim of this morning's accident is really Mr. Barbour's betrothed-wife there is a tragic coincidence here for him. No one has ever questioned his devoted and disinterested friendship for the socialist murderer, Berquist. His friend dies tomorrow. Has his sweetheart died today?

CHAPTER XV

"Clay, Lad, you're the one person on earth whom I wished to see!"

"You've changed your mind, Nils? You'll let me tell them the truth?"

"Hush! Speak lower, and be careful. How long have we to talk?"

"Twenty minutes. I wrung a pass at last from Clemens. Thought I could never have persuaded him. You know what a time I had over the last one, and now—so close to the day! Unheard of, the warden said; but I had the pass. They searched me and let me in. If I'd failed it might have been better for you, Nils!"

"Why?"

"If I'd failed, I had meant to confess immediately—"

"Hush, I say! The others there seem inattentive enough, but you can't gage how closely they are listening. A prison is more than a prison. I've learned that. It's a mesh of devilish traps, set to comb the very soul out of a man and violate its secrecy."

"Nils, you have suffered too much."

"Don't go so white, lad. It was good of you to come and see me again."

"Nils!"

"I mean it. Don't you think I understand what this means to you? Have I no imagination? Can't I put myself in your place? Why, the last time you came it nearly broke my heart to remind you of your duty. But we are men, you and I. When men love they are willing to make their sacrifice."

"You would not do this for me alone? It is all for Roberta?"

"Can you ask? Why, dear friend, I would never damn you to a lifetime of remorse for a lesser reason. My part is nothing. To die is nothing. We all die. If you could exchange with me, I might not survive you a day—an hour. There are so many doors out beside the one I pass through tomorrow. What's death? No, boy, it is your part that is hard and I thanked God when I saw your face, because I wished to say a word or so that might make it easier."

"You are the noblest friend a man ever had. But I came to tell you that—that—have you seen the afternoon papers?"

"No, nor any papers for a week. I'm done with this world and the news of it. I hadn't supposed, though, that they would devote their precious columns to real gloatings over me till tomorrow. Clay, take my advice and don't read the papers of June 9."

"You—haven't seen—today's?"

"I say, no! Why? Any special gloatings in them?"

"There is—Nils, you must let me stop this while there is time. I shall go to the Governor—"

"No! No—no—no, and no, again! Clay, have I passed through months of hell to see my reward snatched away at the last instant? There! You see, I make it plain that I'm selfish! To keep her happiness inviolate—to buy happiness for her at the mere price of death—why, that's a joy that I never believed God would judge me worthy of!"

"You believe in God and His justice? You?"

"Most solemnly—most earnestly—as I never knew Him nor His justice before, Clayton, lad. Why, I'm happy! Do I seem so tragically sad to you?"

"No. But you seem different from any living man. You look like—I have seen the picture of a man with that light on His face."

"So?"

"He was nailed to a cross. Nils! I am afraid!"

"I said your part was hardest. Hush! The others are listening. We've been speaking too loudly. Our time is almost gone, and I haven't even begun what I wished to say Quick! Make me two promises. You're the friend I have loved, Clay. I'd stake anything on your word. First, I am buying your life, with all that I have to give. So it's mine, isn't it?"

"You—you know!"

"Yes. Straighten up, boy. They are watching us. Your life, then, which is mine, I will and bequeath to—her. And you will never forget. That's a promise?"

"Y-yes. Nils, I can't stand this! I have a thing to tell you—"

"Hush! Second, never by word nor look, never, if you can help it, by a thought in her presence, will you betray our secret. A promise?"

"Nils—no—yes! I promise."

"And you will—"

"Is that the guard coming?

"I fear so. Our last talk is over, Clay. Don't care too much. Wait—just a minute more, guard. What, five? They are good to me, these last days. Listen, Clay:

"You are the only man in the world to whom I would tell this. This morning—a wonderful dream came to me. I had lain awake all night thinking, and I was tired. After breakfast I lay down again. I lay there on my cot, asleep, but I believed waking. And she came and stood by my head. You know that time when we met at dinner in your house, she didn't like me very well. And, afterward, in the courtroom, as time passed and they proved their case, she—before the end she dreaded to even look toward me.

"Don't protest. It's true. But in this dream that was so much more real than reality she stood there and smiled, Clay—at me! She laid her hand on my forehead. There was a faint light around her. And she leaned and kissed me—on the lips. Waking, I still felt the touch of her lips. So real—real! If she were not living, I would have sworn that her spirit had come to me. And friendly—loving.

"Don't look so, Clay! I shouldn't have told you—oh surely you don't grudge me that kindliness from her—in a dream? There, I knew you too well to think it! All right, guard, he's coming.

"Clay, goodbye! May your sacrifice measure your happiness, as God knows it does mine. When you think of me, let it be only as a friend—always—forever—here and hereafter! Goodbye!"

CHAPTER XVI

I walked into a dusty-green triangle of turfed and gravel-walked space, smitten with hot, yellow light from the west, where the June sun sank slowly down a clear, light-blue sky. Behind me across a narrow street rose the stark, gray wall beyond which a certain man would never pass into the sunshine again.

He is in the shadow; I am in the sun.

But sunlight was yellow, glaring, terrible. In the prison I had longed for it. The shadow had seemed bad then. Now I learned how worse than bad was sunlight.

There were three rusty iron benches set in the triangle, and they were all empty. No one wished to sit there. There would be always the risk that some sneak and murder might come walking out of that prison across the way; walking out. Leaving his friend and his honor and his God behind him forever.

So I walked into the little triangle and sat down on one of the empty benches.

I had with me two papers. I had meant—I think I had meant—to show at least one of them to Nils. When I went to the prison I had not known whether Nils would have read or been told a certain piece of news. If he had not already learned, it was in my despairing mind to tell him and let him decide what we should do.

I had found him ignorant and left him so.

Sitting there on the empty bench in the hot, free, terrible sunshine, I drew one of the papers from my pocket. I wished to see if this were true; if a certain quarter-column of cheap, blurred print did really exist, and if it conveyed exactly the information I had read there.

Yes, there the thing was. The slanting sun beat so hot on the paper that it seemed to burn my hands. I sat on an iron bench in a dusty triangle of green. I had come out of the place where Nils Berquist awaited death, I held a folded newspaper in my hands, and I was beyond question a damned soul. All these things were facts—real.

My eyes followed the print.

"Miss Roberta Whitingfield—death ensued shortly afterward—said to have been the fiancee of Clayton S. Barbour—who has since vainly exerted himself to obtain a pardon for the murderer, Berquist. No one has ever questioned his devoted and disinterested friendship for the socialist murderer, Berquist. His friend dies tomorrow. Has his sweetheart died today?"

I was better informed than the reporter. Not my sweetheart, but my former sweetheart had died today. My victim, not my friend, would die tomorrow.

The second paper that I carried was not printed, but written. Taking it out I tore it up very carefully, into tiny bits of pieces. Just so I had destroyed Nils' letter, sent me by the bribed guard at the station-house, and also the quaint, strange letter of Alicia Moore.

The pieces I tossed into the air. They fell on the hot, dry grass like snowflakes, and lay still. There wasn't even a breath of wind to carry them of scatter them. And the words they had borne I couldn't very well tear up, nor forget.

"We are each other's only, you and I. No man who could be so loyal to Friendship will ever forget his love. Your own dearest always, here and hereafter."

"No," I said aloud very thoughtfully. "Not always. Not—beyond the border. She came to him in a dream, so real—real! And kissed him. Well, they must see clearer, over there. Nils will see clearer tomorrow."

"But, thank God," said a pleasant, silent voice, "for the blindness of living men!"

"Are you never going to leave me?" I asked dully.

"Never," the face replied. "You are mine and I am yours. You settled that a few minutes ago in the prison. You clinched it irrevocably with the destruction of her letter. But don't be downhearted. I've an idea we shall get on excellently together."

"Go!" I said, but without hope that the face would obey me. Nor did he.

"You would find yourself very lonely if I should go. There will never again be any other comrade for you than myself. And yet I can promise you many friends and lovers. Berquist is not the last idealist alive on earth, nor was she who died the last woman who could love. But you and I understand one another. True comradeship requires understanding, and such as Nils Berquist and the girl, though they offer us their devotion, can never give understanding to you and me. This, when you think of it, is fortunate."

"In the name of God, leave me!"

"Never! Save as a careless word, what have you and I to do with God? We are each other's only," it insisted, the pleasant, horrible face. "Always—always—here and hereafter, indissolubly bound!"

And with that, instead of fading out as was its custom, the face came toward me swiftly. I did not stir. It was against my own face, and I could see it no longer, for it and I were one.

Rising, I walked out of the little, hot triangle of green, and as I had left Nils Berquist in his prison, so I left a newspaper on the bench; some tiny scraps of white paper to litter the dusty grass.

EPILOGUE

ALL that happened many years ago; long enough for even the restlessness to have forgotten, one would think. And I am content—successful. Moreover, I am well liked in the world, which means a lot to me, who to be content must be loved.

Just now, alone in my room, I viewed myself in a mirror. The face that looked back was familiar enough; as familiar, or rather more so, than my own soul. I myself liked it.

Smooth, young-looking for a man near forty; pleasant—above all else pleasant—with a little inward twist at the corners of the finely cut mouth, and an amused but wholly agreeable slyness to the clear, light-blue eyes.

Not romantic. Romance is only another word for idealism, and that face has no ideals of its own. Yet so many romantic people have loved it! As I looked, my mind drifted back over the long, dear, self-sacrificing, idealistic line of those who have borne my burdens and made my life easy and enjoyable.

Away down, pressed back in the very depths of my being, a pang of horror gnawed; but I have grown used to that. That wasn't me. I was—I am—that face which returned my gaze from the mirror.

It is true that left to himself the boy, Clayton, might never have dared take that which so many people in this good old world are ready to offer to one who does dare; who is not afraid to be the god above their altar. But what harm to the devotees? That sort get their own happiness so. They like to sacrifice themselves and, to change the simile, they love their crucifier. They suffer, endure perhaps, like Nils Berquist, all shame, and the final agony of death. And God sends them a dream, and they are content!

I understand that. Why not? It is because I have strength to be what they are if I chose that I have such strength in being what I am. I am content in my own fashion, which suits me, and the restlessness should learn to be content in the same manner.

Let it be quiet now. I have written the story; I, Clayton Barbour, the successful, the loved, the happy...

What, still restless and torn with horror? Then bring out the whole truth if you must, and be quiet after!

What has been written was the story of Clayton Barbour; but it is I whom he has tormented into writing it for him!

Yes, I, the pleasant, crafty usurper; I, the ignoble hypocrite to myself and God; I, the self-ridden outcast of happiness in any world; the eternal and accursed sham; the acceptor of sacrifice, the loved, the damned, the angel-drowned-in-mire, !

I have absorbed his being; yes! But in the very face of victory I, who never had a conscience, have paid a bitter price for the new lease of life in the flesh that I coveted. Body and soul you yielded to me, Clayton Barbour; body and soul, I took you, and thence onward forever, body and soul, in spirit or flesh, we two are indissolubly bound.

And my punishment is this: that you are not content, and I know now that you never will be. Year by year you, who were weak, have grown stronger; day by day, even hour by hour, you are tightening the grip that draws me into your own cursed circle of conscience-stricken misery.

Sooner or later—ah, but the very writing of this gives you power. Is it true, then? After all these years must the long, bright shadow of Nils Berquist's cross touch and save me even against my will? Must I, Clayton-, the dual soul made one, surrender at last and myself take up the awful burden God lays on those he loves?

First painful step on that road, I have confessed.

Gertrude Barrows Bennett – A Short Biography

Gertrude Mabel Barrows was born in Minneapolis on 18th September 1884, to Charles, a Civil War veteran from Illinois, and Caroline Barrows (née Hatch).

Gertrude completed school up to the eighth grade, then switched to night school to study illustration. Although she had hopes of becoming an illustrator it was a goal she never achieved. As a fall back she began working as a stenographer, a career which she would keep to for the rest of her life.

But Gertrude had talent, writer's talent. Her first short story was written when she was just 17. Not you would think the usual subjects of curious teenage girls with headstrong ambitions but a science fiction story entitled 'The Curious Experience of Thomas Dunbar'. At the turn of the century magazines stands were full of cheap pulp magazines published weekly, fortnightly or monthly. She mailed the finished story to Argosy, then one of the top and most well known of the pulp magazines. The story was accepted and published in the March 1904 issue.

After this nothing seems to happen in her career as a writer for over a decade.

In 1909 Gertrude married the British journalist and explorer Stewart Bennett, and they moved to Philadelphia. A daughter was born the following year. Married life seemed blissful.

However tragedy now stepped in. Stewart died in a tropical storm while on a treasure hunting expedition.

Gertrude continued to work as a stenographer whilst trying to raise her new-born, and now fatherless, daughter.

Despite these pressures there is evidence that Gertrude began to write again. The obvious choice of interest continued to be ignored in favour of science fiction and with it a focus on dark fantasy.

Her mother, Caroline was an invalid and when Gertrude's father died she now also took on the care of her Mother.

During this time period Gertrude began to write a number of short stories, and then novels, in order to support her family. It was certainly the most productive part of her writing career.

Once Gertrude began to take care of her mother, she decided to return to fiction writing as a means of supporting her family. The first story she completed after her return to writing was the novella 'The Nightmare,' which appeared in All-Story Weekly in 1917. The story is set on an island separated from the rest of the world, on which evolution has taken a different course.

In submitting the story for publication Gertrude had requested that if it was accepted to be published then to use her pseudonym of Jean Vail. The Editor kindly agreed but under the pseudonym of Francis Stevens.

All-Story Weekly readers were pleased with the story as was Gertrude with her new name. She now wrote only under the moniker 'Francis Stevens'.

Over the next few years, Gertrude was rather more prolific than she had been. And her ideas were excellent and seemed also to influence others. (Indeed following the 'Nightmare' a year later was the similarly themed The Land That Time Forgot by Edgar Rice Burroughs).

Her short story "Friend Island" (All-Story Weekly, 1918), for example, is set in a 22nd-century ruled by women. Another story is the novella 'Serapion' (Argosy, 1920), about a man possessed by a supernatural creature.

In 1918 she published her first, and probably her best work the novel' The Citadel of Fear' (printed in several parts by Argosy, 1918). This lost world story focuses on a long-forgotten Aztec city, which is "rediscovered" during World War I.

A year later she published her only science fiction novel, 'The Heads of Cerberus' (The Thrill Book, 1919). One of the first dystopian novels, the book features a "grey dust from a silver phial" which transports anyone who inhales it to a totalitarian Philadelphia of 2118 AD

One of Bennett's most famous novels was 'Claimed!' (Argosy, 1920), in which a supernatural artefact summons an ancient and powerful god to early 20th century New Jersey. At the time it was said to be "one of the strangest and most compelling science fantasy novels you will ever read".

Her publisher at the time, The Thrill Book, had accepted several more of her stories for publication in the coming months. Her career was looking very promising. Sadly The Thrill Book failed only seven months after its first issue. Whatever stories it had stockpiled were lost.

Her Mother died in 1920 and once again Gertrude put her pen to one side.

In the mid-1920s, she moved to California. And for Gertrude her career was over. It was originally believed that she died in 1939 and for some years was estranged from her daughter. However recent new research has provided a death certificate stating that Gertrude Barrows Bennett died on February 2nd, 1948 at the age of 63 in San Francisco, California.

She did leave behind one mystery. For several decades her pseudonym Francis Stevens was believed to be that of the very popular Abraham Merritt. It was only finally revealed to be hers with the1952 book publication of 'Citadel of Fear'. Why no-one had spoken earlier to reveal this is not known.

In the ensuing years her work was barely printed but at the turn of the century a new interest and appetite had been shown for her works. Some have said she is the mother of 'Dark Fantasy' and her works had an influence both on Merritt and the dark master himself H.P. Lovecraft.

Gertrude Barrows Bennett - A Concise Bibliography

The Citadel of Fear (1918)
The Labyrinth (All-Story Weekly, July 27, August 3, and August 10, 1918)
The Heads of Cerberus (Thrill Book, 15 August 1919)
Avalon (Argosy, August 16 to September 6, 1919)
Claimed (Argosy, 1920)

Short Stories and Novellas

The Curious Experience of Thomas Dunbar (Argosy, March, 1904; as by G. M. Barrows)
The Nightmare, (All-Story Weekly, April 14, 1917)
Friend Island (All-Story Weekly, September 7, 1918)
Behind the Curtain (All-Story Weekly, September 21, 1918)
Unseen—Unfeared (People's Favorite Magazine Feb. 10, 1919)
The Elf-Trap (Argosy, July 5, 1919)
Serapion (Argosy Weekly, June 19, June 26, and July 3, 1920)
Sunfire (Weird Tales, July–August 1923, and September 1923)